RAINING
SARDINES

raining sardines

enrique flores-galbis

a deborah brodie book
ROARING BROOK PRESS
new milford, connecticut

A Deborah Brodie Book
Published by Roaring Brook Press
Roaring Brook Press is a division of Holtzbrinck Publishing Holdings Limited
Partnership
143 West Street, New Milford, Connecticut 06776

Library of Congress Cataloging-in-Publication Data

Flores-Galbis, Enrique.
Raining Sardines / by Enrique Flores-Galbis. — 1st ed.
p. cm.
"A Deborah Brodie Book."
Summary: The artistic Ernestina and the analytical Enriquito use their
ingenuity to save a herd of wild horses and stop an evil landowner from
spoiling their Cuban village.
ISBN-13: 978-1-59643-166-9
ISBN-10: 1-59643-166-0
[1. Horses—Fiction. 2. Cuba—Fiction.] I. Title.
PZ7.F66433Dan 2006
[Fic]—dc22
2005036205

10 9 8 7 6 5 4 3 2 1

Book design by Michael McCartney
Printed in the United States of America
First edition March 2007

To Laurel Ives, Olivia, and Mia,
my inspiration and encouragement.

I am grateful to
Gareth Esersky,
Rosemary Stimola,
and Deborah Brodie,
three publishing professionals
super endowed with *El Rayo X*.

A mi madre,
Raquel Flores-Galbis,
estas siempre cerca.

"Ernestina,

there is a lot of strange stuff in the water today."

For two days, the big storm had danced the *rumba* in their bay. She left tired fishing boats resting on their sides, palms teetering on crates, and a three-legged chair standing defiantly in the seaweed.

Enriquito perched next to Ernestina at the end of the pier. Ernestina she wasn't listening. She was somewhere over the horizon, riding cloud ponies with their white manes flying.

"Ernestina, *mira!* A big pink thing is floating this way!" Enriquito pointed upwind, where the running sea met calm bay waters. "I think it's a boat."

Ernestina reluctantly let go of the wind and floated back to the old stone pier. She watched a crew of shipwrecked crabs frantically scampering over the rolling shape. Then four legs popped out.

"Enriquito, that's not a boat, it's a big pig! He must have drowned in the flood—there's another one!"

"Ernestina, that's not a pig—it's a couch."

A gust of wind brought them a woman's voice, warm and rich, singing:

> *En Agua Clara se puede ver*
> *los misterios al fondo del . . .*
> In clear water one can see
> the mysteries at the bottom of the . . .

The wind shredded the song into little threads and blew it away.

"*Mira*, Enriquito! There's a lady sitting on the couch!"

They dropped their fishing lines and ran out to the end of the pier. The bounding couch was no more than five feet away from them.

"Ahoy there, and how are you today?" the lady called out.

Enriquito looked around for a scrap of rope or a long pole, but the storm tide had swept the pier clean.

"She's floating out to sea!" Ernestina yelled.

Enriquito counted, "*Uno, dos, tres*," and they jumped into the wild green sea.

"It's so lovely to see you." The woman patted the cushions on either side of her. "Right on time! Welcome."

Ernestina and Enriquito climbed aboard, and before

they could say a word, she announced theatrically, "I am Clara!"

Enriquito squinted at her suspiciously. Ernestina could think of nothing to say, which was unusual for her.

"They called me *Aguas Clara, la Divinadora*. Clear Waters, the Great Seer."

They had never heard of her.

"My father and I used to sail this coast, bringing a glimpse of the future and sometimes the past for those who desired it."

Enriquito and Ernestina were still mystified. Clara explained, "You could say that I was a floating fortune-teller.

"The stories of my miraculous powers to see and make accurate predictions spread from Pinar del Rio to Oriente Province. People who had never met me spoke of me as if I were a work of fiction, a product of someone's imagination. But, after sitting with me for five minutes, they knew—I belonged in the nonfiction department of their brains." Clara laughed and adjusted the open collar of her light brown velvet robe. Her fingers drifted to a gold medallion cut in the shape of an eye, hanging from a string of cowry shells around her graceful neck. She wore a bracelet made of the same light-colored gold.

Her skin, the color of *café con leche*, a creamy light brown, was the same color as the robe and the couch. It was almost impossible to tell where she and her robe ended and the couch began. If it weren't for the aqua-blue fabric wrapped around her head, she would have completely disappeared.

On her lap, a teapot teetered on a tray. In her hand, she held a steaming cup.

"Oh my, how rude of me! I apologize. May I offer you some tea? Although I know for a fact it is not your favorite drink. As you can imagine, I left the house rather hastily this morning. I didn't bring any Pepsi or ice."

Enriquito and Ernestina looked at each other. How could Clara know that Pepsi was their new discovery, over ice on a hot day, filled all the way to the top of the glass so that the bubbles tickled your nose as you sipped it slowly?

Ernestina felt the cushions and poked her toe into the waves that carried them along. She was making sure this was not one of her vivid daydreams. After all, a lady sailing by on a floating couch was tame compared to some of the fantasies she created to entertain herself.

"Yes, Ernestina, I am real." Clara laughed. "And if it can rain sardines, why can't a couch float?"

As the couch bounded along the mouth of the bay, they could see the new chalk line that the *carnival* wind had drawn for the beach. Behind it, the mountain sloped down to the bay, cupping their village in palm-covered hills.

Clara settled deeper into the cushions. "My father and I used to stop at your village. The people were happy—

I could tell by the funny, uncomplicated questions they asked. The young girls wanted me to tell them about the man they would marry. Would he wear a mustache, or have a limp? The women asked about the next episode of their soap opera. The men just wanted the winning lottery numbers." Her laughter rocked the couch.

"There was one man who was very different, whose story might interest you." Ernestina wondered why the story would interest them. Clara patted Ernestina's knee, and said, "You'll see, *querida.*" Then she adjusted the fabric rising like a shiny seashell above her head.

"I had spent the day sitting in the shade of the almond trees in your lovely town square, answering hundreds of questions about boyfriends with mustaches, lottery numbers, and lost goats. It was early evening when I looked up and saw a line of people still waiting to see me. I was tired, but I could not disappoint them, so I promised we would stay one more day. That evening, Father tied up our little houseboat at the village dock. We ate our dinner and then, as usual, started on our never-ending game of dominoes. Right about midnight, there was a knock at our door."

Clara rested her teacup on the top of Enriquito's head as naturally as if it were a dinner table. "When my father opened the door, a tall, handsome man stepped into the cabin of our little houseboat. He was wearing a suit that was well pressed but very much out of style.

"My father greeted him. The man did not speak; he looked past him—straight at me." Clara took a sip of her tea. "Those wise brown eyes had seen more than one life." She carefully set her cup back on Enriquito's head.

Her hand danced up to the medallion, down to her wrist. She tapped her bracelet three times. In the hypnotic rhythm of a lullaby, she whispered softly, "Deep in his eyes, I saw it all at once: his past, the present, and his future. Images flowing, clear as water."

She raised her hand. "Clear as water, images flowing," Clara intoned softly.

Enriquito stared at the lines on the palm of her hand, swirling free, then spiraling into a dark liquid, flowing into the hollow of her hand.

"Yes, Enriquito, I am holding night in my hand. Look inside, what do you see?"

Floating puddles of light gather. A moonbeam, bright as a circus spotlight, catches the corner of an open door inside a courtyard. Something is crawling out of the inky shadow of the room, slithering across the tiles like a big black snake. The gate to the courtyard opens. A sliver of moonlight knifes across the floor, over the crawling shape. The shape freezes for an instant, gathers itself, and then stands. It is not a snake. It is a thin little man, dressed from head to toe in nothing but a layer of shiny black grease. The greased man looks straight at Enriquito.

Then a tall man carrying a sack jumps through the

gate into the moonlight. He throws the sack, it clangs into the dark corner, and he dives for the greased man. The tall man wraps his arms around the slippery little man, but he pops out of his grasp and runs into the corner. There is a dull thud, a metallic clang, and then someone wheezes, "Gold!"

"Who sent you?" the tall man bellows. "Speak, or I'll knock your head off!"

The little man is sliding across the tiles on his belly, trying to squeeze into a tiny drain hole at the bottom of the wall. The tall man grabs his legs and tries to pull him back. The greasy thief squirms through the hole and disappears. The tall man runs into the room off the courtyard. He comes out, his face bleached white by a shock of moonlight. "He's gone!"

Clara's voice gently calls Enriquito back. "I saw the event in his past that changed his life. I felt the great weight of the secret he was carrying."

Enriquito blinks, the lines settle into the palm of Clara's hands, and night retreats.

"I promised I would help him," Clara said, "help him pass along his secret to the right person—when the right time comes. The next morning, I found this strange gold necklace and bracelet hanging on my door." She held them up. "This gold has also seen many lives. If you listen, it will tell you a story or two!"

Enriquito studied the eye on the medallion. Tight

little spirals with long curving tails radiated out to form the eyelashes. On the bracelet, the same little spirals were woven into a pattern of vines and leaves.

Clara lifted her teacup, patted Enriquito's head, then cupped his chin in her hand. He could feel her eyes, the color of the sea over a shallow sandbar, looking right through him, as if *he* were clear as water.

With the tip of her finger, she traced a swirling shape in the center of his forehead. Enriquito heard her say, "One to forget, two to remember." Clara smiled and winked at him. "Believe in your dreams. When the right time comes, if you listen, you will hear me."

Then she reached for Ernestina's hand and closed her eyes. She threw her head back and laughed. "*¡Mi hija!* You are so full of color and light. It's so strong. Never be afraid of it. Don't let anything or anyone smudge that color or put out the light."

Enriquito checked the direction of the wind, and stuck his toe in the water to feel the strength of the current. "We are drifting out to sea!"

Clara lifted her head and peered over the back of the couch. A lone fishing boat, with its sail full of wind, was heading into the bay. As it sailed closer, Clara called out to the fisherman, "Romero, *marinero sincero*, come closer."

The fisherman changed his course, and soon the bow of his boat was nudging the cushions of the couch.

Clara greeted the fisherman as if he were an old

friend. "*Hola*, Romero, I'm glad to see you've had a good day of fishing."

The fisherman sat at the tiller with his glistening catch slithering around his knees. He did not seem a bit curious about the fact that a strange lady, floating by on a couch, was calling him by his first name. He tossed them a line. "You better hold on to this."

Clara helped Enriquito and Ernestina stand up on the springy cushions and then jump across to the fishing boat. They found a place to sit at the bow of the writhing boat, then reached out to help Clara aboard.

Clara sat back, smoothed out her robe, and announced, "I thank you very much for the offer, but I am sailing on to Havana."

Suddenly, the invisible blanket of silence lifted. "Clara!" The sound of their own voices surprised them.

"Now, now, children. There are big changes coming soon, and the people in Havana are going to need all the help they can get."

The wind picked up and the fishing boat strained against the rope. She let it slip through her fingers, and they began to drift apart. As the fisherman turned his boat toward the village, the distance between them grew.

Enriquito yelled, "Come back, Clara!"

"I will, *viejito*. Just look for me, I'll be there." She waved and called out, "Havana by sunrise!"

Then Clara, the couch, and her words all blew away in a gust of wind.

Enriquito let himself slide down into the slimy belly of the little sailboat.

The fisherman, chewing on the stump of a cigar that he planned to light when he got back to the dock, was looking at the flagpole on the village dock. The Cuban flag, flat out in the fresh breeze, snapped brightly. Her red triangle and blue stripes looked like they were tacked to the sky.

The fisherman raised one finger into the breeze and said, "With this wind, she'll be in Havana *before* sunrise."

Long, syrupy shadows were creeping across the road when they finished helping the fisherman unload his catch.

"Ernestina, what do you think all that stuff about listening and dreaming means?" Enriquito asked.

"If she really is a fortune-teller, it means that something is going to happen."

"What's going to happen?" Enriquito asked.

"You are not supposed to know, because if you did, it wouldn't happen."

Enriquito swatted at a mosquito buzzing in his ear. "That sounds mysterious, like something a grown-up would say."

Ernestina pinched her nose to imitate her teacher's voice. "Someday, it will all be as clear as water."

The mosquito was now singing in his other ear. "Ernestina, if you say it'll make sense later on, I can wait."

Ernestina dreamed that her mother and Clara were sitting on a couch floating in and out of a pink sea mist. At one moment, they were blurry pink and far away; at the next, they felt touching-close. Clara was speaking to Ernestina's mother in a language Ernestina could not understand. Her mother, waving for her to come and join her, drifted into pink, and then they disappeared.

Ernestina tossed and turned all night.

In the morning she was like a sleepwalker, with one foot in the fog of her dreams and the other in the dusty day.

Her mother had left early to catch the first bus to Havana. Ernestina stood in the middle of the kitchen staring at the large cup of *café con leche* with a small plate covering it to keep it warm. A *cangrejito*, a crab-shaped pastry, crawled across the note on the plate.

> *Querida,*
> I'll try to be back for our *merienda.*
> > *Muchos besitos,*
> > Mama

Ernestina spilled *café con leche* on her leg and watched it dribble into her droopy sock. She stuffed the *cangrejito* into her shirt pocket, tied her books up in an old leather belt, and headed for school.

Alysia Rigol-Betancourt looked down her thin little nose. "Ah, here is Ernestina, our own little peasant in her little peasant skirt."

This was the skirt her mother had lovingly sewn for her, the only skirt she owned, the skirt she had worn every single day that year.

Alysia Rigol-Betancourt had fine birdlike hands and smelled of violet soap. She wore an ancient gold locket that her grandmother had given her, and ivory combs in her flowing blond hair.

On the very first day of school, she had spotted Ernestina flopping down the hall. Alysia stood in the middle of the hallway, studied her for a moment or two, and then delivered her verdict.

"Let's see now: fingernails cut too short—she probably chews them. Her shirttails hanging out— doesn't even know it. Her hair hasn't been brushed in days—a perfect place for a bird's nest."

The girls gathered around Alysia snickered.

"Perhaps I should not be so hard on her. Perhaps she is from some other land where this is their idea of beauty."

The girls laughed and complimented Alysia on her wit.

Then, speaking very slowly as if Ernestina might not understand, Alysia asked,

"What country . . . are . . . you . . . from?"

"What do you mean, what country am I from?" Ernestina shot back. "I'm a Cuban, just like you are."

Ernestina's response startled Alysia. No one had ever dared talk back to her like that.

Alysia puffed herself up, and said in her haughtiest tone, "Like *me?* You will never be like me. My family has been here for three hundred years. We own your little street and probably the little house you live in. My great-grandfather built this school so that girls like us wouldn't have to mix with peasants like you!"

Ernestina shifted her books to her left hand and took a step toward Alysia. But she stopped abruptly when she saw her mother's face, floating just above Alysia. The face, her mother, was talking to her, repeating what she had said the morning of her very first day of school. "Ernestina, I know how those girls are, they are going to tease you and try to make you feel bad because you are not like them. Just smile, act like it doesn't matter. Don't ever forget why I moved mountains to get you into that school."

How could she forget? In her old school there were no art classes, no art room with bouquets of brushes arranged like flowers in a vase, no fat tubes of paint packed in their drawers, no large white canvases waiting to be painted.

Ernestina had gathered herself and walked past the girls as if they were of no more consequence than flies on a screen door. Then she'd stopped and turned around. "You are right," she'd said. "I'm not like you. I am Ernestina." Then she'd walked off to her first class on the first day of school.

All year long, she had brushed off Alysia's comments. She had never complained to the teachers when Alysia tried to trip her as she walked by her desk. She had learned how to step over and around every mean trick that Alysia could think of.

Sometimes she wondered if it was worth all the stomachaches just to be able to paint every day. But then she would walk into the art room, smell the paint, grab a brush and, when the colors began to flow through her fingers, nothing, nothing could touch her.

But today, her hands felt as big as baseball mitts, her feet like clumps of dirt, and her hair as coarse as a thatched roof. Today, she didn't have the strength to laugh it off.

Alysia Rigol-Betancourt had finally worn her out, convinced her that she didn't belong in this school.

A thin gray cloud passed over her face and smudged her features. She lowered her head and shuffled past the laughing girls.

The day went by in a gray haze. Finally, the last bell rang and she slipped out of school, kicked off her shoes, and ran down the packed-sand road.

Enriquito waded through the flock of red-and-white chickens pecking in the schoolyard. The black rooster and his blue shadow strutted by in the stinging sunlight. If anyone got too close to his ladies, he would strike, his red crest waving like a battle flag. His razor-sharp talons rarely missed their mark.

At the crossroads, Enriquito scurried to his lemon tree, checked for ants, and then slipped into the shade. He tried to keep as still as the lizards dozing above him among the lemons and the thorns. Today, the breezes that usually sweep the heat away had gone to sweep elsewhere. Enriquito felt as if he were sitting in a green oven.

Ernestina came whistling down the road in full view of the angry sun. She was swinging her books into the weeds, trying to imagine a cool day.

"Ernestina, aren't you hot?"

"I'll be better when the rain comes."

"Rain?" Enriquito asked hopefully.

Spinning slowly in the middle of the crossroads, Ernestina was shimmering in the heat waves. "Enriquito! It's coming. Can't you feel it?"

Then, as if they had been waiting for her signal, sparkling little raindrops came tinkling on a fresh breeze.

Ernestina closed her eyes and turned to face the cooling spray.

"Aah! The coolness! It feels like I have chilly blue dots all over my face."

Suddenly, a wall of angry brown clouds surged up from behind the mountain and waves of rain swept across the peak, blurring its outline.

In no time at all, the sprinkles turned to fat raindrops that rolled and then popped in the dust. Enriquito took off his shoes and splashed through the little rivers in the road.

They heard the first clap of thunder, looked up, and saw a neon finger of lightning pointing at the face of the mountain. "Warning number one!" Enriquito yelled.

The rain was now falling in slanting sheets. It looked as if the ocean, tired of its seabed, had risen up to walk the land and rearrange things.

Land crabs the size of Chihuahuas hustled out of their flooded holes and marched up the center of the road. Lizards and iguanas splashed through puddles as snakes slithered by.

Suddenly, a flock of gulls swirled low overhead and the bottle-green air breathed a school of glittering fish. Ernestina danced and squirmed as sardines got tangled in her hair. She shrieked. "Enriquito! It's raining sardines!"

Little fish flickered and slimed inside Enriquito's shirt. "Fish can fly and couches float," he giggled.

"Clara, *La Divinadora*!" Ernestina crowed.

A second thunderbolt crackled overhead. "Warning number two!" Enriquito shouted, and started running home.

Ernestina picked the last sardine out of her hair as she swung through her front gate.

She ran up the front steps, hurried inside, and called out, "Mama, are you home?" Her voice searched the quiet house and then echoed back, alone. She changed out of her uniform and went into the empty kitchen.

When she saw the green plate with the caramel candies stacked on the note, she knew. Her mother's plates were white with a blue band. "Why today, of all days?"

She had looked forward to having *merienda* with her mother. Sitting at the kitchen table, drinking lemonade, and talking about her school day.

Ernestina grabbed the note and an empanada, then marched out through the screen door. When she got to the old shed in the backyard, she stopped in the doorway to read the note.

> *Ernestina querida,*
>
> Your mother sent word that she will catch the late bus and be home to give you *un besito* before you go to bed. Please come and have *sopa de pollo* with us tonight.
>
> *Señora* Maruri

"That's the second time this week." Ernestina folded the note and stuffed it into a coffee can with the others. "Papi is in Havana all the time and now Mami too."

Enriquito's mother hugged Ernestina and hummed. "Tonight we are having *sopa de pollo* with the thin little noodles, just as you like it," *Señora* Maruri said as she ladled the steaming soup into a bowl and handed it to Enriquito. "Be careful now, it's very hot."

Enriquito pressed his face close to the bowl, searching out the peas. He always ate the peas first, the noodles, and then the potatoes. Right before he tipped the bowl up and drank the rich broth, he ate the thin pieces of chicken. As he ate, he peeked over the lip of the bowl at Ernestina. She was lost in thought.

Enriquito cleared his throat and said, "Don't you want to tell us a story, Ernestina?"

"Do you remember the last time you ate with us?" *Señora* Maruri asked. "You started to unwind one with the soup, and then reeled it in while we washed the dishes. That was some story!"

"Sorry," Ernestina mumbled into her soup. "I can't think of one tonight."

Enriquito went back to hunting for peas. The *click* and *clack* of the spoons were the only sounds to be heard in the kitchen.

Señora Maruri put her hand on Ernestina's shoulder. "*Querida*, I know your father is in Havana all the time and now your mother too. You must miss them. You want your family to be together, but sometimes parents have to go far away to work—that's important."

She reached over to Enriquito and squeezed his hand. "Enriquito's father has been away now for six months. At first it was really hard for both of us. I felt like a three-legged table—all wobbly."

Enriquito piped in, "I thought Papi was gone because I had done something wrong."

Ernestina looked at Enriquito as if he had just said something brilliant. "I've been thinking the same thing," she admitted.

Señora Maruri gave her a little smile and said, "I'll tell you exactly what I told Enriquito. There is nowhere in this world your parents would rather be than with you, together, as a family. There is nothing you have done or haven't done that caused them to go. The sad fact is that, right now, in this town, there is no work for them. And if they don't work, you don't eat. That's the way life is. But don't worry, because whatever flies apart always comes together again. Soon everyone will be home all the time, we'll play dominoes on the porch like we used to, talk and laugh all night long."

Ernestina looked up from her soup. Enriquito and

Señora Maruri were smiling at her through the steam rising from their bowls.

The cloud over her head started to lift, rising higher, until the whirring blades of the fan swept it away.

At the place where the howling jungle seemed intent on swallowing the road, Ernestina and Enriquito found the break in the foliage. They waded across a stream, wiggled into a green child-sized tunnel formed by the branches of a fallen tree, and came out at the edge of a small meadow.

The deep banks of the stream circled the meadow like the moat of a castle, keeping most intruders out.

They sprinted to a large, head-shaped boulder in the center of the meadow, climbed up the cheek, and sat down on the temple.

A green skirt of sugarcane fanned out below them, the white lace of waves showing where the sea hemmed the fields. Alysia's family owned the land from the meadow down to the shore.

The Rigol-Betancourts had arrived three hundred years ago with the Spanish General Velazquez and his army of conquistadores, to claim the land for Spain. Ever since then, they had been growing sugar, raising horses, and telling people what to do.

Sometimes, Enriquito and Ernestina would make believe they were Tainos, living in the jungles of their green mountain. They could see the Spaniards, riding up the mountain on their sure-footed Paso Finos. This small, sturdy breed was famous for its smooth gait. This was important to the armor-clad Spaniards. If they tried to sneak up on the Tainos on any other horse, their armor clanged and clattered like pots and pans rattling down a hill.

Not too long after they stumbled into their secret meadow, Ernestina and Enriquito discovered a small herd of Paso Fino ponies. Direct descendants of the conquistadores' horses, they lived wild and free, high up on the mountain, venturing down occasionally to eat the sweet grass that grew only in the meadow.

Over time, Ernestina and Enriquito were able to get close to these rare creatures. It was a privilege that came with a great responsibility. They knew that if anyone else found out about the herd, the ponies could never roam free again.

Enriquito stood on the boulder and whistled until his face turned as red as a cooked lobster. He whistled the way his father had taught him, the whistle that only horses could hear.

Soon, they heard the muffled sound of hooves in the jungle. The rustling of the foliage announced the entrance of the young stallion. He stepped cautiously into the clearing, sniffed the wind, and when he was sure there was no danger, whinnied softly. One by one, the herd appeared. First, two younger stallions, the old mare, a yearling, then the filly pranced in last.

The herd meandered slowly along the edges of the clearing until they were downwind from Ernestina and Enriquito. When the horses recognized their scent, they lowered their heads and began to graze on the sweet grass.

The stallion circled the herd nervously as they munched closer and closer to the boulder. Ernestina and Enriquito climbed down slowly from the rock. If they slipped or jumped down, the ponies would panic and run away. They waited for a moment in the shadow of the rock, and then began to walk, side by side, toward the herd.

Enriquito placed a carrot in the palm of his hand and extended it slowly toward the ponies. The filly picked up her head and came forward to meet him. Without hesitation, she began to nibble on the carrot. Her silky muzzle tickled Enriquito's hand. Ernestina gently stroked the filly's face. The rest of the herd gradually gathered and formed a circle around them.

The stallion never let down his guard. He nervously paced around them, occasionally nipping at the ponies, reminding them to stay alert.

Ernestina handed Enriquito a blanket. Speaking to the

filly in a soft, calm voice, he began rubbing her neck with the blanket. "Good girl, good filly." He slowly worked his way to her shoulders, then the middle of her back.

The filly swung her head around to look at Enriquito as he slowly unfolded the blanket. He was about to lay it across her back, when the stallion reared up to give a blood-curdling alarm.

The ponies pricked their ears toward the downhill side of the meadow, sifting the breeze for a sound or a scent. The nervous stallion began to round up his herd. Finally, Enriquito and Ernestina heard pounding hoof-beats and the loud cracking of branches as the bushes at the edge of the meadow shook wildly.

Alysia Rigol-Betancourt crashed into the meadow, clinging to the mane of a black stallion. Seeing it had room to run, the powerful horse put down its head and galloped even faster over the sweet grass. Alysia was screaming at the top of her lungs for someone to save her.

Ernestina climbed to the top of the boulder, crouched down like a panther and prepared to leap. As the horse and rider flew by, Ernestina jumped across the spooked animal's back and grabbed Alysia. They tumbled off the running horse onto the meadow, their fall cushioned by the thick carpet of grass.

Enriquito tried to drive the Paso Finos back into the jungle. They ran wildly around the meadow once, with their long manes streaming behind them, then thundered out through the small opening in the jungle wall.

Alysia was now up on one elbow, watching them disappear into the jungle. "Did you see that? Those were the wild ponies." She dusted off her riding jacket and said, "They are on my property, I claim them." She looked down at Ernestina, who was still on the ground, and said, "You are on my property too! I should have you arrested!"

Enriquito was bending over Ernestina, trying to help her up. Ernestina calmly thanked Enriquito and picked herself up. Although she was wearing a short-sleeved T-shirt, she made the motion of rolling up her sleeves as she marched over to Alysia Rigol-Betancourt.

Enriquito saw what was coming, and fell in like a shadow behind Ernestina. Just before she got to Alysia, Ernestina stopped, took a deep breath, then cocked her head, like a bird sizing up a bug for a meal. In her chilliest teacher's voice, she said, "Those ponies don't belong to you. They've been living on this mountain, wild and free for hundreds of years. They could never live in a corral!"

"Ernestina, I am sure you know that the meadow, this mountain, and everything living on it belong to my father. As a matter of fact, I heard him say that he's going to clear the jungle from the farm up to this meadow, to plant coffee beans. So where will your precious wild ponies live then? It will be a good thing to bring them in from this wilderness," Alysia gloated.

Ernestina was surprised to hear her say that the mountain belonged to the Rigols. Everyone knew that it belonged to the town. This was also the first time she had heard about the coffee plantation. This did not worry her too much. Even if they cleared up to the meadow, the ponies would still be safe because they would have the rest of the mountain to hide in.

"Alysia, you self-centered little snob, did you not notice that we just saved your life? If we had not been here, that horse would have fallen down into the stream, and both of you would have broken your necks."

Suddenly, Ernestina sounded as if she were about to cry. "All year long, you made fun of me and tried to make my life miserable at school just because I'm not rich and fancy like you and your friends." Enriquito's ears perked up. "You never even tried to get to know me!" Ernestina finished with a theatrical quiver in her voice.

This sounded like the old Ernestina. Enriquito knew she was up to something. She was getting ready to play Alysia like *el Viejo*, the Old Man, played the big fish, fish so powerful that they could swamp his boat with one slash of their tail. To Enriquito it sounded like Ernestina was giving Alysia some slack, waiting for something she could use to set her hook.

Enriquito tugged on Ernestina's sleeve and whispered in her ear. She raised her eyebrows and a wicked little smile crossed her face. Then she said sweetly, "My friend

Enriquito has just told me that the stallion you were riding is your father's prized Arabian, which rarely leaves the stables. I'll bet he is worth more than all the boats in the harbor and all the houses in town put together. I wonder what your father would say if he knew that you were riding him in a place where most people wouldn't take a donkey.

"Tell me, Alysia, just how do you plan to catch that horse and bring him home? Do you think he is just going to stand there and let you get back up on him?"

Alysia gave Ernestina a defiant look and started walking toward the stallion. She did not get more than twenty yards away from the stallion when he bolted and ran wildly around the border of the meadow.

"Oh, Ernestina, do something! He's going to step in a hole and break a leg," Alysia pleaded.

Ernestina winked at Enriquito. Enriquito whistled so hard that his cheeks bulged like two ripe tomatoes. Enriquito whistled so hard and high that they could not hear it. This was the secret horse whistle his father had taught him. Almost like magic, the stallion slowed, and then stopped.

"Now go get him, bring him to me," Alysia commanded. When Enriquito and Ernestina did not move, she added grudgingly, "Please?" Alysia scrunched up her face as if the word had left a bad taste in her mouth.

"On one condition," Ernestina said. "Promise that you

will tell no one that you saw the wild ponies. You see, if you catch them and bring them in, they will not survive. They can't be owned."

"Are you telling me that I can't have something that is rightfully mine?" Alysia said in her usual haughty tone.

Ernestina looked at her and then slowly turned around and began picking up her things as if she were getting ready to leave.

"Where are you going? You can't just leave me here. I order you to stop! *Stop!*"

Ernestina did not turn around.

"Oh, please don't go." Alysia sounded desperate.

Ernestina, and now Enriquito, kept walking toward the edge of the clearing.

Alysia pleaded across the meadow, "Oh, Ernestina, you don't know how mad my father will be if he finds out. He loves that horse more than he loves me. Please help me!" Then, having a hard time getting the words out, she said, "I promise I won't breathe a word about the ponies."

Ernestina turned around and said, "What did you just say? I couldn't quite hear you."

Alysia repeated it a little louder, in a very annoyed tone. "I promise I won't say anything about the ponies."

Ernestina slowed down, but did not stop.

Then Alysia said, "You know, Ernestina, the only reason I was mean to you was because you are not like the other girls. You are strong and confident, I couldn't boss you around like the others. Until the other day, I couldn't even make you mad. I'm so sorry, Ernestina."

Ernestina stopped just as she reached the tunnel that led out of the meadow. She turned and looked at Alysia's face. It was no longer cold and haughty. Even in her wildest dreams, she had never imagined she would ever see Alysia Rigol-Betancourt cry. Her natural reaction was to go back and give her a hug and make her feel better. Instead, she reminded herself that it was still Alysia Rigol-Betancourt she was dealing with. Ernestina turned her heart into a stone.

"Why should I believe you, Alysia? Why should I trust you?" Ernestina turned and crouched as if to enter the little tunnel.

"Wait. Don't go." Alysia unfastened the clasp of the locket her grandmother had given her. She gently slipped it off and held it lovingly. "My father gave this locket to my grandmother. I heard him say that it's made from a special kind of gold. It is very, very valuable. It means a lot to me because my grandmother gave it to me before she died. I loved her with all my heart because she loved me, no matter what. Take it, as proof that I intend to keep my word. I will never tell anyone about the ponies—you can keep it until you are sure that the ponies are safe." Then she solemnly handed the golden locket to Ernestina.

Like a general receiving the keys of a conquered city,

Ernestina held it in her cupped hands and said, "Alysia Rigol-Betancourt, I accept this as a token of your word and give you mine that if anything happens to those ponies, I will tell your father about the stallion and you will never see this locket and chain again."

"We'll see. I mean, I understand," Alysia said.

Enriquito returned with the stallion following behind him like a big dog. He was looking at the sky, which had filled with heavy charcoal-colored clouds, and said, "If we don't hurry, we are going to get wet." He saw the locket around Ernestina's neck and came in close to inspect it. Ernestina held it up for him to see. The glowing gold would not let him look away. The locket felt warm in his hand.

Just then a lightning bolt split the sky and struck the boulder. An ear-shattering bang immediately followed. The stallion reared up and raked the air with his hooves, just missing Alysia. She was trying to crawl out of the way when it reared again and almost crushed her with his mighty hooves.

Enriquito leaped at the stallion's head and clamped his arms around it. The surprised stallion lurched back and spun around, with Enriquito hanging on tight. He stretched as far as he could, pulled on the stallion's ear, and bit it. The stallion shrieked and tried to buck Enriquito off, but Enriquito bit harder. The stallion spun around once more and then suddenly stopped.

Enriquito whispered something into the stallion's ear and he calmed down.

Alysia got up and ran to Enriquito's side. "I have been around horses all my life and have never seen anything like that before!"

Enriquito looked down at his dirty sneakers and said humbly, "My father taught me."

He handed Alysia the reins, just as it began to rain.

"Quick. Help me up," Alysia commanded.

Enriquito put his hands together; Alysia stepped into them and swung herself up into the saddle.

The rain was falling. Alysia, her wet hair drooping over her face, was looking down at them. She didn't seem to know what to say. Ernestina was enjoying the moment. "Don't forget, Alysia, we've got a deal." She held out the locket—their prize.

"Put that thing away, you fool, don't let it get wet. It better be in good condition when I get it back!" Alysia yanked on the reins and the stallion spun around.

She hit him once with her riding crop, and they thundered out of the meadow.

The girls in Sister Theresa's history class were sitting with hands folded, feet together, looking straight ahead like little angels. Ernestina slouched in the last seat of the last row, sifting through the cobwebs on the ceiling.

Ignacio, town historian and poet, stood next to Sister Theresa's desk, his head tilted as if listening for words whispered in the wind. His fingers hovered over the polished wood of the desk. His eyes rolled upward as if he were inspecting a painting on the ceiling only he could see. "Hatuey, the wise leader of the Taino people . . ."

The girls sighed and then settled into their uncomfortable chairs. Ignacio told the same story every year. Every child on the island knew that story by heart.

The singsong rhythm of Ignacio's voice washed over Ernestina. His words floated above her, the cobwebs swirled and then opened to reveal a starry tropical sky.

Young Hatuey stood with his arms outstretched, feet firmly planted, looking up at a yellow moon. Siboneys and Arawaks gathered around him in a great circle, on the shore of a long, narrow lake.

"I have crossed the waters, my brothers and sisters, to warn you of a great danger approaching. A cruel invader has come to our island and caused great suffering among us.

"At first, I thought them to be gods because they are so different from us. But I have been told that one of them drowned in the river.

"It is hard to believe that they are human beings like us. I have never known men to be so heartless." Hatuey paused as the families around him whispered. "I think they are men, driven mad by the God of Gold." Hatuey turned his handsome face up to the moon and then back to the frightened tribes. "Since it is the gold that makes them behave so strangely, we must get rid of all of the gold we possess. Then the curse on these men will be lifted. And we can live in peace again."

He removed a band of gold from his arm and tossed it into the large basket that had been placed in the middle of the circle.

A great shout went up, the drummers answered the call. Men, women, and children threw their gold into the basket as they danced by.

Hatuey picked up the basket of gold, raised it over his head, then sang his prayer:

"God of Gold, please accept our gifts and deliver us of this evil that is upon us. God of the Lake, please accept our gift. Fierce cayman, son of the lake, guard this treasure bravely."

Hatuey heaved the basket as far out into the lake as he could. Then the three tribes danced to the drum and the echoes of their prayers.

The moon descended to the far side of the room, and the rising sun painted the ceiling pink and green.

Suddenly, an inky black stain seeped into the pink of the new day. *Crack!*

Ernestina's dreaming eyes tried to focus on the blurred

forms moving in front of her—the wooden yardstick, the bony hand. Her eyes climbed up the black tower of itchy fabric to Sister Theresa's face. "You are an embarrassment to this school!" Sister Theresa hissed at her. Then she politely addressed Ignacio.

"Please excuse the interruption, our class daydreamer seems to have drifted off again."

Somewhere, far off in a dark hallway, a bell rang.

Sister Theresa held Ernestina at her desk, pressing the yardstick down hard on her shoulder. "Little dreamer, you must learn to stay in the present and pay attention, otherwise you will have great difficulties in life."

When she released her, Ernestina mumbled to the desk, "Thank you, Sister Theresa," then headed for the door.

Halfway across the room, Ernestina stopped and turned around. "With all due respect, sister, I was paying attention. I was listening so hard that I saw pictures moving on the ceiling."

Sister Theresa spun around like a black twister. It was terrifying to see someone her age move so fast. Her eyes bulged, honing in on Ernestina. "Pictures on the ceiling? I'll show you pictures on the ceiling!"

For some reason, everything Ernestina said or did irritated Sister Theresa. The nun didn't like her and that was that.

Ernestina did not wait for the stick or the lecture. She ran to Ignacio, who was standing by the door, and grabbed his hand. She was hoping Sister Theresa would not whack her in front of the honored guest.

"An artist's hand and a poet's heart." Ignacio said. "It must be Ernestina!"

Ernestina glanced back at the charging nun, then blurted out, "Thank you for coming in to talk to us, Ignacio."

The poet gently guided her by the hand out to the hall. Then in a soft, kind voice, he said, "Never apologize for dreaming. After all, where would we be if we could not dream?"

Ernestina found Enriquito on *L'il Havana*, with his face pressed close to the mast, studying the brass fittings on the deck. She jumped down, a little off-center, and the boat rocked wildly from side to side. Enriquito lost his balance and bumped his head against the mast.

"Hey! That hurt!" Enriquito howled.

"It's lucky you've got a hard head. Is the mast okay?" Ernestina joked, trying to make him laugh.

Enriquito slipped into the little cabin where they stored the anchor and net.

"I guess you have every right to be mad at me. You can stay in there as long as you like, but we still have to get bait for *el Viejo*. We did promise him."

Ernestina chattered while she got *L'il Havana* under way.

"With the wind blowing into shore and the tide going out, we're going to get a lot of chop. If I were a slimy little mackerel, I would swim near the surface because the birds can't see very well into choppy water."

Ernestina set the sail and then turned around to check their wake, to make sure she was sailing true, just like *el Viejo* had taught them. When she looked back at the town and the mountain rising behind it, she yelled, "Enriquito! You better come up here and take a look at this!"

"I've seen them." Enriquito had already noticed the columns of black smoke rising to the right of the town.

"Enriquito, the smoke—they're clearing the jungle to plant coffee beans. I didn't think they were going to get that close to the meadow! The ponies—they'll never be safe again!"

Enriquito climbed out of the cabin and looked back at the land. "If the ponies get captured, it will be our fault."

"What do you mean?" Ernestina screeched. "How could that be our fault?"

Deep down, Ernestina knew that every time they visited the ponies, they became a little less fearful. Their fear had kept them free for all these years. She knew this all along, but she loved being with the ponies.

"Oh, Enriquito, I feel terrible. We have to do something!"

Enriquito gathered the net as Ernestina swung *L'il Havana* out of the wind.

"Ready with the net?" she called out.

Enriquito leaned into the rail to steady himself. He cast the net and then watched it drift down into the blue. "There is only one thing we can do."

"I know, we can't go see the ponies anymore," she said.

"Yes. But we can't leave things as they are. We have to put everything back the way we found it." Enriquito gently tugged on the net. "If we just stop going to visit the ponies, they'll still come down to eat the sweet grass. Sooner or later, someone will see them."

Ernestina could picture the Paso Finos, fear flashing in their eyes, trying to find their way out of the meadow. A circle of men drawing closer, tightening the noose that would steal their freedom.

Enriquito felt the net getting heavier. He waited for it to fill and then tugged on the line as hard as he could to close it. Ernestina leaned in and they hauled up the net together.

"Enriquito, we have to find a way to scare those ponies from tame back to wild. We have to give them such a scare that they'll never come to the meadow again."

The rising net took the shape of a large bowl. The fish, leisurely swimming inside, were unaware of what was about to happen. As the net got closer to the surface, the bowl got smaller and the movements of the fish more frantic. By the time the net reached the surface, it was a flashing mass of frightened fish.

Ernestina was staring deep into the water. "Enriquito, I think I just saw the answer," she blurted out.

Enriquito loosened the slipknot that kept the mouth of the net closed. Fish slithered and thumped on the deck as they tried to leap away.

"We have to get the ponies back in the meadow, make them feel trapped, scare them, and then let them escape," Ernestina said.

Among the snappers and the mackerels, they found two large sea horses. Enriquito filled two buckets with seawater. He slipped the mackerels and snappers into one bucket, and the sea horses into the other. "*El Gringo* will pay us two *pesos* each for these beauties." He threw the fish they didn't want back into the sea.

They sailed across to the eastern tip of the bay, tied *L'il Havana* to a rusty iron ring driven into a rock, and clambered up to *el Gringo's* house.

El Gringo had been coming down to fish in their bay for years. The moment he set foot on this spot, he fell in love with the idea of building a house on the rocks.

They found *el Gringo* surrounded by workmen on the second floor.

He towered above them as he joked and gave instructions. Standing next to him was a distinguished-looking gentleman wearing a white linen suit, holding a new Panama hat, lovingly, in his hands.

Enriquito studied the stranger and whispered to Ernestina, "I'll bet you my penknife that he is from Havana."

They walked quietly to the large aquarium set into the wall, already filled with colorful fish.

"Ernestina! Enriquito! Good to see you. I'll be with you in a moment," *el Gringo* called to them.

He slapped a few backs and sent the workers off into the house. Then he and the stranger sauntered over to them.

"I'd like you to meet my *compañero* and fishing buddy from Havana, Chief Magistrate Cardenas."

The stranger extended his hand and said, "Ah! *Los pescadores*, my friend has told me a great deal about you and your sea horses. It is an honor to meet you."

El Gringo looked into the bucket and said, "What a beautiful pair! Very good, let's put them in!" He carefully scooped the sea horses out of the bucket with a net and gently placed them in their new home. They darted about and then headed for a large piece of coral at the very center of the aquarium. *El Gringo* laughed. "Two new citizens for our floating world."

One of the workers called him from the stairway. He handed Ernestina four pesos. "There you go, as we agreed." When he noticed Enriquito studying the brass telescope at the window, he added, "Stay as long as you like. *Adios, amigos.*" Then he and the chief magistrate disappeared up the stairway.

Enriquito stepped away from the telescope. "Ernestina, take a look at this." The powerful telescope brought the green mountain close enough to touch. Under charcoal-gray veils of smoke, huge chunks of cleared land were creeping up the mountain like a brown flood.

The townspeople had seen the smoke and the glow of the fires, but when the curtain of clouds lifted, they realized just how much of the mountain *Don* Rigol was taking for his coffee plantation.

The mountain, where they planted their gardens, and the children played, had always belonged to the town.

As soon as the rain stopped, the square began to fill. At first, they gathered in little groups, fishermen in one corner, farmers in another, townspeople and merchants by the stage. A group of families, surrounded by a sea of bundles, was camping under the trees. The families had been living on the mountain until Rigol's men kicked them off.

The men were hanging back in little clusters. The women walked away, forming their own group—*someone* had to speak to *Don* Rigol. Then they held up their wooden spoons, ready to make some noise beating the pots and pans they had brought from home.

The mayor, a roly-poly little man in a wool suit, stepped into the middle of the group. He suggested that perhaps it would be better if they took a more diplomatic approach first. If that did not work, then they could beat their pots and pans as much as they wanted to.

The mayor slipped through the crowd to the merchants' group. He whispered and pleaded, shook some hands, then returned to the women to present his case.

With as much authority as he could muster, the mayor announced that the merchants were the ones best suited to deal with *Don* Rigol, since they knew how to talk and negotiate.

The mayor picked out eight men from the group of merchants and herded them toward the women. He puffed himself up and declared, "As the mayor of this town, I hereby authorize this fine committee to investigate the matter at hand."

As the eight men set off for the Rigol-Betancourt plantation, one of the women shouted to her husband, "Tomás, if you don't get results, you don't get dinner!"

The mayor's committee arrived at the front gate of

the Rigol estate two hours later, dusty and thirsty. They politely announced their business to the gatekeeper, who looked at them with a mixture of pity and scorn. His son was sent to the big house to ask if they should be allowed in.

They waited for what seemed like hours. Finally they spotted the boy, walking lazily from one side of the road to the other, stopping to trap a sleeping lizard or two before he reached them. He ran the last ten feet to his father, and whispered something into his ear.

The gatekeeper, with a smirk on his face, slowly opened the gate. In a voice dripping with false sincerity, he wished them, *"Buena suerte, amigos,"* and laughed.

The floors of the grand house were red, black, and white marble laid in a diamond pattern, the walls paneled in a dark mahogany. A spiral staircase floated in the center of the immense room. They noticed the expensive oriental carpet at their feet. Not wanting to scuff it up, they tiptoed along the black marble border of the floor.

The merchants stood with their hats in their hands, shyly peeking at the marble columns and sneaking an occasional feel of the velvet curtains.

They heard someone barking out orders from deep inside the house. Two servants rushed into the foyer, rolled up the carpet, hoisted it onto their shoulders, and hustled it off to safety. No one offered the men a cool drink or a place to sit.

Finally *Don* Rigol, Alysia's father, appeared at the top of the stairs. He descended halfway down the spiral staircase and stopped to adjust the cuffs of his silk shirt. "Gentlemen, what important business brings you such a great distance to my humble home?"

The committee was silent.

"Perhaps you have forgotten to choose a spokesman to articulate your concerns. Please do so quickly, I am a very busy man."

There was a buzz of whispers and they all turned toward Alfredo, the owner of the bait shop. He reluctantly stepped forward, clutching his hat, nervously rolling and unrolling it until it was a shapeless mass of straw.

"*Señor*, we are here to say that the people are very upset with what is happening to our mountain. We knew that you were clearing some land to plant your coffee beans, but now it seems as if you intend to clear the whole mountain. We think that you are taking for yourself something that belongs to the people of the town. We love that mountain. We don't want to lose it."

Don Rigol took one more step down toward them and said in a self-pitying tone, "How can I ever bring progress to this area if I have to drag along, kicking and screaming, the very people who will benefit from this progress? Why are you people so backward, so shortsighted?"

Don Rigol sighed. "The coffee brings jobs. Jobs bring money. People with money buy things from the merchants.

That money ends up in your pocket—isn't that what it's all about?"

Then, with his temper rising, he said, "I cannot help the fact that you believed the myth that the mountain belongs to you. It is a nice fairy tale, but gentlemen, this is the real world. In the real world, real men rely on fact, not on fairy tales." He pulled aside his green velvet jacket and reached into his shirt pocket, pulled out a piece of paper, and ceremoniously unfolded it. It was too far away for them to see what it was. For all they knew, it could have been a shopping list.

"This, gentlemen, is fact. This deed is a legal document that shows that our property extends all the way to the very top of the mountain. The whole mountain is Rigol property. This fact is officially recorded in book number 17. You will find this book at the records office in the town hall. I suggest you go there and verify what I have said." He scanned the group cowering in his foyer. "That is, if you can read."

"One last point. The Rigol family has always been, right from the beginning, the driving force in this town. We established the bank, where you get the loans to run your businesses. We built the roads you travel on every day. We built your library and the town square where you read and relax." *Don* Rigol trained his black snake-eyes on each member of the committee.

"I am sure you understand how upset I would be if I

felt that our good townspeople, who have benefited from our generosity, were ungrateful."

He clapped his hands twice; his foreman and three big cane cutters entered the room and surrounded the group.

Don Rigol climbed the stairs, then turned and said, "Gentlemen, it is always a pleasure." He snapped his fingers and the committee was herded out of the grand Rigol-Betancourt mansion.

As the grinning gatekeeper slammed his gate shut, he called out, "Please come again." His laughter followed them on their long, sad walk home.

When the dusty men finally dragged into town, Enriquito and Ernestina were sitting in front of Garcia's, sipping cold lemonade. They slipped from the shadow of the building into the shadow of the committee.

In the records office, Ignacio and his assistant, the nephew of *Don* Rigol, greeted them.

Ignacio, sensing an unusual number of people in the room, asked how many were present. The assistant answered, "Twelve."

"Oh my, we don't get twelve people here in twelve months, much less all at once. How can I help you?" Ignacio asked.

The tired merchants explained that they needed to see the map in book number 17.

Ignacio turned to where the young man had been standing and asked him to get the book.

The young assistant placed Ignacio's hand on the shiny leather-bound book and said a little impatiently, "There it is, right in front of you."

A few of the men laughed. Alfredo, their spokesman, dropped his bushy eyebrows and scowled at them.

Ignacio's fingers skimmed across the soft leather, and then he said, "Yes, number 17. By the way, gentlemen, I am not offended by your laughter. I've had plenty of time to get used to my limitations."

The committee admired the hand-painted emblem on the cover, a circle with a Paso Fino and a royal palm in the center. The gold-leaf background looked like it had been recently painted.

They crowded around the open book, studying the notes and descriptions of fences and boulders that marked the property. They checked the number of the map and asked Rigol's nephew if he was sure that this was the right one. They took turns tracing the boundary lines with their fingers and looking at each other in disbelief. There it was, map number 17 in black-and-white, the fact *Don* Rigol had spoken of.

The Rigols owned the mountain.

Enriquito had snaked his way inside the mass of

sweaty men. He squeezed his head in between two extra-large bellies in order to get a clear view of the book.

Ernestina, at the far end of the counter, could see into the small room where the record books were kept. The back wall was lined with wooden shelves groaning under the weight of the big, dusty books. Ernestina noticed that among the old books with torn covers and loose pages, there were a few that looked shiny and new, just like the one on the counter. Like leather school shoes in September.

The men of the committee could think of nothing else to say or ask, so they slipped out of the office. Ernestina and Enriquito followed in their wake.

The mayor was stirring the fourth teaspoon of sugar into his *café con leche* when they came into Garcia's. He knew the committee would need refreshments after their long walk. "Well, you checked the records and I assume you found that everything is in order?"

Julio, the man who sold ice, spoke first. "I can't understand it. According to the town maps, they own the whole thing."

The mayor reached across the table and patted Julio's shoulder.

"Sometimes we have to weigh things. Sometimes we must pay a price in order to gain. That coffee plantation will put money in your pockets. We must not forget that we are lucky to have *Don* Rigol making things move in this town. They do many things that benefit us. For instance, when you needed money to start your ice business, where did you go to borrow it?"

Silence fell over the group. They did not need him to explain. If *Don* Rigol said the sky was red, then the sky was red.

The mayor stood up and announced, a little too cheerfully, "We will have a meeting in the town square, and afterward, a certain citizen, who wishes to remain anonymous, has made funds available to hire a band and buy refreshments."

There was only one citizen in this little town who could afford to provide refreshments for all.

The stage at the center of the square was crowded with musicians, the committee, and the mayor, sweating in his wool suit.

"Ladies and gentlemen, we should all be proud on this day for having acted in a truly democratic fashion," the mayor huffed. "This fine committee carried out their civic duty honorably. We are thankful to these fine men who asked the hard questions and did the painstaking research. Unfortunately, according to the maps, *Don* Rigol owns the mountain, all the way to the top."

A man in the back of the crowd yelled out, "That land has always belonged to us!" Others in the now angry crowd agreed.

The mayor raised his hands and gave them a stern look. "Who told you that the mountain belonged to you?"

The man in the back thought for a moment and then answered, "My mother." Other voices joined in, calling out, "My father," "My uncle," "My teacher." A kid in the back yelled, "My dog." The crowd laughed.

The mayor raised his hands. "These fine men of the committee went to the records office and saw the map that proves *Don* Rigol's claim. It is unfortunate how rumors get started and handed down, but in this case, the truth is on paper, a fact for all to see." Then he spread his arms as if he were about to hug the whole crowd. "We must respect the books and follow the law."

The crowd was a buzzing, angry beehive.

The mayor yelled out, "Quiet! Settle down! I understand how you feel, yes I do. I know this is unfortunate news, but we are fortunate in another respect, and if you let me speak, I can give you the good news. A certain citizen has made a generous contribution so that we can finally build the market building we have needed for so long. This generous benefactor has also made possible tonight's entertainment and the refreshments." The crowd was thrown off balance by the good and bad news.

The mayor did not wait for the crowd's response to the news. Before anyone could get organized, he spun around and waved at the band. The musicians raised their instruments and jumped into an upbeat dance version of "*Guantanamera*," the most popular song in the land:

Yo soy un hombre sincero
De donde crecen las palmas
Ante de morirme quiero
Echar mis versos del Alma.
I am an honest man
From where the palms grow
Before I die I want
To let the verses fly from my soul.

The verses were written by José Martí, Ignacio's favorite poet. He often told the story of Martí's arrest and exile, recounting the details of his tragic death soon after he returned to free his beloved Cuba. Ignacio liked to finish by saying, "José Martí, born a poet, died a patriot!"

Trumpets and drums drowned out the questions that were still being hurled at the mayor. The women shook their skirts and swayed to the main beat of the drum, while the men cocked their heads like roosters and moved to the beats in between. The silent beats you feel in your backbone.

¥¥¥

Enriquito and Ernestina squeezed out of the crowd to find *el Viejo*, leaning against a tree, observing the scene. "Are you walking up the hill?"

Ernestina and Enriquito fell in step with the old

fisherman on the road to the top of the hill that over-looked the harbor. They came to a large tree shading a crumbled wall. "Let's rest here," *el Viejo* said.

Enriquito plunged into the tall grass to follow the remnants of the wall that had encircled a once grand house. The walls of the house were crumbling; there were gaping holes where the windows had been. Shoots and vines grappled with the railings, pulling on posts as if they were trying to drag the house back into the jungle. The floor tiles, with their hand-painted designs, mimicked the leafy vines that slithered across the floor.

Enriquito liked to sit quietly in the courtyard, the heart of the house, and listen. Sometimes he heard muffled voices seeping through the walls, like conversations in other rooms. The voices were strangely familiar, but he could not understand what they were saying. Something had happened in this courtyard—he could feel it.

El Viejo and Ernestina were sitting in the shade, look-ing down at the people in the square. The wind breathing through the trees carried the sounds of the fiesta out to sea. Without the music, the dancers looked like frantic little ants knocking into each other.

"If it weren't so sad, I would laugh," *el Viejo* said, shak-ing his leathery head.

"What do you mean?" asked Ernestina.

"It is sad to see people dancing to forget."

"Forget what?" Ernestina asked cautiously.

"Things that they can't do anything about."

"What things?" Ernestina knew she was not going to get a direct answer. Ever since he had given up fishing and moved to his shack on the hill, *el Viejo* had taken to answering questions with questions, and leaving sentences and people dangling.

El Viejo looked up into the jungle. "My father was a woodcutter."

"*Ay, Dios.*" Ernestina sighed.

"He and I worked up in the jungle, cutting mahogany. There used to be a lot of mahogany trees up there. People who build ships and fancy buildings love mahogany. It is a beautiful wood and almost as hard as my father's head."

Ernestina was about to burst. "What does your father's head have to do with people dancing to forget?"

El Viejo smiled at Ernestina. "You want me to get to the point, I suppose."

"Please," she pleaded.

"Well, one day, a pack of Rigol's men came into our camp. They announced that we were trespassing and, on orders from the landowner, *Don* Rigol, we had to leave immediately. My father didn't like that one bit. He had grown up on this mountain; he knew who owned every rock, tree, and snake on it, and it wasn't Rigol. They threatened to drag us out if we didn't leave on our own.

"I remember my father standing there with his big

double-edged ax in his hands, smiling at those hired thugs. I'll never forget what he said."

The Old Man reached into his memory for his father's voice. "I cut mahogany, the hardest of woods, from sunrise to sunset. My blade never dulls and my arms never tire. If any of you want to test the steel of my blade and the iron in my arms, you are more than welcome."

El Viejo recited his father's words as if they were carved in mahogany.

"I imagine *Don* Rigol's men all had families that they wanted to see at the end of the workday, so they backed down. As they were leaving, the head man leaned in close to my father and said, 'You are a good man. I would hate to see you get hurt. You should know that *Don* Rigol wants this mountain and he will stop at nothing to get it.'

"When we got back to town, my father and I went directly to the town hall to check the record books.

"At that time, Ignacio was the assistant clerk. He was a law student, working at town hall for the summer. This was before he lost his sight.

"He went into the little room in back and brought out a very old book with a worn black leather cover. The map we looked at was old but it was very clear that the town owned the land all the way to the top of the mountain, not *Don* Rigol. I remember it well.

"My father knew that the Rigols were planning to take the mountain for themselves and he wasn't shy about telling anyone who would listen. I was there when *Don* Rigol himself came to see him. He warned him that terrible things happen to people who spread false rumors.

"The next time we went up to cut, they were waiting for us. They attacked us while we slept. There were too many to fight off, but my father didn't go easy. They hurt his arms badly and he was never able to cut mahogany again."

"Is that when you became a fisherman?"

"Yes, I had no choice, the family had to eat."

"I don't understand." Ernestina looked puzzled. "We snuck into the records office and saw the map with our own eyes. On that map, the land all the way up to the top of the mountain belongs to the Rigols."

El Viejo didn't seem surprised. "Sometimes things are as plain as the nose on your face."

Ernestina sensed he was slipping back into mystery. "What is as plain as the nose on whose face?"

"The way things are," *el Viejo* responded. He looked her in the eye and said, "They dance to forget because of the way things are."

Just then Enriquito came running back. "Hey, what are you talking about?"

"Dancing and forgetting," Ernestina said glumly, and started walking up the hill.

"Do you remember what the house looked like?" Enriquito asked *el Viejo*.

"Your great-grandfather's house? Sure, I remember. There's not much left of it now. That was one of the nicest houses in town. Everyone was welcomed there.

"Your grandmother, your mother, and her uncle Aurelio, the jeweler, lived there after your great-grandfather disappeared.

"I was there the day my father, your great-grandfather, and Aurelio left to go look for treasure up on the mountain. I would have gone too, but the fishing was too good to miss. I was there the day Aurelio came back alone, scared out of his wits. My father and your great-grandfather were never seen again. Aurelio was never the same after that."

"They never came back? What happened to them?" Ernestina asked. "Enriquito, did you know about this?"

"My mother told me that her *abuelo* had gone hunting on the mountain and never came back. The only one who came back was *Tio* Aurelio. After that, he never left the house. That's all she's ever said about it."

Ernestina faced *el Viejo.* "Could you answer a question? Just a simple question? Why couldn't he tell anybody what happened?"

"The only person who could have answered that simple question never spoke another word. When Aurelio died, the family had to sell the house. *Don* Rigol was the only person who could afford such a large house. He made the first and only offer. Aurelio would roll over in his grave if he knew how little *Don* Rigol paid for it.

"*Don* Rigol went in with his workers and they took that house apart, piece by piece. He was there every day, watching them tear down walls and dig up the floors—as if he was looking for something. He took it apart and never put it back together again."

When they arrived at *el Viejo*'s shack, Enriquito asked, "What do you think *Don* Rigol was looking for?"

"Enriquito, that's a long story and it's not mine to tell. I am sure your mother will tell you all about Aurelio's history when she is ready."

They watched a freighter steaming into the bay to pick up a load of sugar. She was empty, riding high. A crimson stripe of rust, the waterline, floated just above the blue-green sea. Tomorrow, she'd be loaded down with sacks of raw sugar, and the red stripe would disappear beneath the waves.

Ernestina was drawing a view of the meadow as it looked from the entrance of the little tunnel. A few shadows made with the side of the charcoal stick, and their boulder appeared. Thin lines flicked on with the tip, and the ponies had their sweet grass to eat. The dark smudge at the edge of the meadow was the break in the foliage where the ponies entered.

"This is where they are going to come in. We have

to be able to close off that entrance quickly. We need a special gate that they can't see on their way in."

Enriquito picked up her charcoal and a piece of white chalk. He drew lines that started on either side of the entrance and curved back down to the ground—he put two dark hatchmarks there. "I'll cut a bunch of those springy little saplings with the thorns that grow behind our houses."

"Right, we'll stick one end in the ground and bend them back as far as we can and tie them down. You have to figure out the knot, something that you can pull on and then it lets go. The saplings will snap up and the gate closes," Ernestina said. She rubbed her nose absentmindedly, leaving a black smear along the ridge.

"I know just the knot I can use," Enriquito said.

Ernestina drew what looked like four plumes of smoke at each corner of the meadow. "The next step is a little trickier. Horses are frightened by anything out of the ordinary. They are very afraid of fire and smoke. We have to make a flash, an explosion with lots of noise and smoke." She drew four more flashes closer to the boulder.

"The ponies usually run around the edge of the meadow when they first come in. We'll set off the ones on the outside and make them run in a tighter circle. Then these"—she pointed at the new plumes—"these will draw them in tighter, and like the fish in the net, they'll get really spooked.

"Remember last year during Carnival when the Devil came out of the mayor's office? There was a big flash and all that white smoke? That's the kind of flash we want."

"We have to go see Ana, the sculptor. She is the one who made the big flash," Enriquito said.

Above the large green doors hung a sign with a carving of a hand holding a pencil drawing an eye.

"This has to be Ana's studio," Ernestina said.

They stepped into the front room and called her name. No one answered. They followed the music, back through a narrow passageway, in between blocks of dark wood, and stones the size of cars. A herd of papier-mâché horses ridden by papier-mâché colonials pranced by, just in from the *Grito de Yara* festival.

Ana had started to carve on some of the stones and the wood blocks. She had chiseled away the surface, as if she were pulling the skin back to see what lay beneath. Ernestina saw parrots and iguanas just starting to emerge from the wood. A powerful horse was pushing its way out of a large piece of marble. Enriquito studied the color and grain of the wood, and decided it was mahogany.

On a long table lay a strange assortment of body parts. Hands carved out of wood, feet of clay, hearts and livers in plaster. Enriquito stopped and inspected the hearts. He picked one up; it felt warm, strangely alive.

"I bet you've never held a heart in your hand before."

Ana stood behind them, her face, hair, and clothing splattered with a white paste. She looked like a little ghost.

"I make those for people who have something that needs to heal. Sometimes it's a broken bone, a bad liver, or even a broken heart."

"Why do you do that?" asked Ernestina.

"To make them better," answered Ana.

"How does it make them better?" asked Enriquito.

"While I make them, I picture the part of the body that's not working right," Ana explained. "Then I picture it healthy, working perfectly. When the person I made it for holds it, they'll feel it too, they'll feel everything I felt while I was making it. I put the heart in it but they make it beat. This is what artists do. We make things that talk to people who want to listen."

Enriquito asked, "What do they talk about?"

Ana spun around. "Come on in! I've got some things in the back, maybe you can tell me what they are saying."

The back room had a very high ceiling with a skylight in the center. Underneath the skylight stood a large shape made of thin pieces of wood that had been wired together.

Ana reached into a big bucket of white paste and

pulled out a strip of cloth. She climbed the stepladder to the top of the shape, the strip of cloth dripping white paste down her leg. "Wheat paste," she said.

"Would you mind handing me the next piece?" she called out, pointing to the bucket at the foot of the ladder.

Ernestina went for it first. She stuck her hand into the large bucket of paste and pulled out another long strip of cloth. It dripped down her arm as she climbed up to hand it to Ana.

"Thanks, *querida*," Ana said as she laid the strip on top of the wood. The shape was starting to resemble a big head.

"Hey! That looks a lot like the mayor!" Ernestina said.

"You've got a good eye," Ana laughed. "Once this dries, I'll paint it, and off it goes. This is going to take three people to carry. Does that say something about politicians, or what!" She joked on the way down the ladder. "Now, what can I do for you?"

This time Enriquito was first. "Well, we are doing . . . er . . . putting on a little spectacle, and we need to make some big puffs of smoke, just like the ones you made for the devil last year. We were wondering if you could help us."

Ana raised an eyebrow. "Spectacle? What do you mean by spectacle?"

Ernestina spoke up before Enriquito really stuck his foot in it. "What Enriquito means is that we want to put on a show for some friends who will be visiting. We really want to impress them, you know, with something they'll never forget."

"And you need the smoke powder, is that it? No problem there, that stuff is safe as dirt. As long as you respect it, it will respect you." Ana walked over to some cabinets in the corner of the room and took out a metal tin.

"How many 'poofs' do you want?" she asked.

"Six will do it," Ernestina said.

Ana carefully scooped out six tablespoon-sized piles and laid them out on a piece of paper. She carefully folded the paper into a square and pressed her hand down flat on it.

Ernestina nudged Enriquito. His hand shot down into his pocket, pulled out four *pesos*, and handed them to Ernestina.

Ana saw the bills and smiled. "I don't take cash, but I do need some studio assistants. I'm up to my ears in work. If you could help me this afternoon, we'll call it even. You never know. You might learn something useful."

Ernestina's eyes lit up. She stuck out her hand and said, "It's a deal."

Ana looked at Enriquito and asked, "Are you in too?"

Enriquito answered, "Yes, please."

The rest of that afternoon, they helped Ana build armatures, like wooden cages, roughly in the shapes of animals and people. At first, they held the pieces of wood together for Ana to join with brass wire. Then she taught Enriquito how to cut the wooden strips to the sizes she needed. Ana let Ernestina place the strips while she wrapped the joints with wire.

Ana howled with delight when Ernestina would name the animal they were making after she had joined just three or four strips of wood together. Once the frames were made, they covered them with rags and paper soaked in the flour-and-water mixture. Ana called it papier-mâché, pronouncing it with a French accent.

Ana dubbed Enriquito the "Master of Plaster." He was in charge of mixing the paste and then dunking the fabric, while Ernestina carefully molded the wet fabric over the armature.

They worked until the light faded to a velvety glow. Ana led them to a large sink and helped them pick the dried paste out of their hair. She softened the globs on their arms and hands with water and gently rubbed them off. As he washed up, Enriquito looked back at the strange parade of characters they had made. "They look like they are about to speak."

"They're probably waiting for us to leave," Ernestina added.

Ana darted away and came back with the packet of flash powder. She handed it to Enriquito. "One tablespoon in the center of a dish or clay pot will do it. Remember, always respect things that fizz and pop."

As they walked through their little town, the afternoon light skidded down the narrow streets, then crashed into the corners.

Ernestina, spinning in the sun-splashed intersection, looked like she had been dipped in honey. "I'm going to be a great artist when I grow up," she said dreamily.

Alysia Rigol-Betancourt broke away from her circle of admirers, and fell in step with Ernestina as she walked by.

"My mother asked me again about the locket," Alysia whispered. "I had to make up a lie to put her off. She wants it back so she can have it cleaned."

Alysia was trying to get out of the deal they had made in the meadow. Ernestina knew that once she gave back the locket, Alysia would not honor her promise, and the ponies would be captured and sold off.

"I can't talk about that now," Ernestina said, and started off toward her next class.

Alysia followed. As Ernestina was about to enter the classroom, Alysia grabbed her arm just a little too hard and hissed, "If I don't get the locket back soon, we will see what we will see. Say hello to those dear little ponies for me." She gave Ernestina her class-picture smile, tossed her hair to the side, and breezed off.

Ernestina knew that, eventually, Alysia would get her way. She had to hold her off until the ponies were safe.

Ernestina woke up right before daybreak. The cottage was still and cool. She could hear her mother in the next room, her breathing peaceful and reassuring, just like the whisper of little waves breaking on the sand.

She dressed and slid like a shadow into the kitchen, and began to gather food for lunch: three empanadas that her mother had saved for her, an old milk bottle filled with sweet lemonade, half a loaf of Cuban bread, and a chunk of *guayava* paste still in the tin.

She slung her burlap sack with the food over her shoulder, tiptoed through the breathing cottage, and then flew down the broad steps.

Just as she landed on the sandy path, the screen door clacked shut, startling the birds in the bushes. Their sleepy complaints followed her all the way to Enriquito's front gate.

Enriquito was checking his list. Clay pots for the flash powder, wire cutters, paints, brushes, containers for water, a bag of flour, and a folding shovel. In a leather satchel tied to his belt, he had a spool of copper wire and a coil of the thin rope the fishermen use to weave their nets.

The night before, they had cut the whip trees and carried them up to the meadow.

They walked silently up the road and into the jungle, crossed the stream, and then crawled through the secret entrance into the meadow.

Inspired by their visit to Ana's studio, they had decided to make papier-mâché figures that would pop up as the horses ran by.

Ernestina arranged the thinnest twigs into the shape of a birdcage for the chest, long tubes for the arms, and a globe for the head. Enriquito held them in place while Ernestina wired them together. When Ernestina finished her figures, they attached them to the springy whip trees that Enriquito had buried along the edge of the meadow. Then they wrapped them, just as they had done at Ana's studio, in plaster-soaked strips of cloth.

Soon they had four figures, rocking back and forth, like sea-legged sailors getting used to dry land.

Enriquito fussed with the ropes and the knots while Ernestina readied the clay pots for the flash powder. She placed them in a circle along the edge of the meadow, then drew them in, in a tight spiral, as they neared the boulder.

"I got the knots just right," Enriquito said, "but you know, I think we are missing something very important."

"What are we missing?" Ernestina asked.

"Smells," Enriquito said. "Horses have a very good

sense of smell. My father told me that horses know you by the way you smell and not the way you look. If you are kind to a horse, he will feel good when he smells you, but if you are mean, he will always remember the fear. We have to attach a smell to the fear so that whenever they smell men, they remember fear."

"You are absolutely right; the solution is stinky clothes, the stinkier the better." Ernestina pulled on Enriquito. "I know just where to get them!"

They ran all the way down to the place where the stream gets wide and deep. As they approached the little clearing, they could hear men shouting and talking. They crept up to the clearing and hid behind a bush. There were eight men in the water. Their deeply tanned faces and arms contrasted with the fish-white skin on their chests.

"It's the cane cutters. They come here every day after work," Ernestina said. "I saw them the other day when I came up here. I'm sure nothing could be stinkier. We could just crawl up to the logs and grab a few shirts. They would never know."

"Yeah, but it's not right to steal their clothes. Those are probably the only shirts they have," Enriquito protested.

"We are not going to steal them. We are going to buy them."

"Buy them?"

"Yes, buy them. We'll leave one *peso* for each shirt. Which is not bad for a shirt that costs only fifty *centavos* at the store," Ernestina said.

Ernestina led the way to the edge of the clearing. Enriquito crawled on his belly out to the closest log, collected six shirts, and signaled to Ernestina. She folded six *pesos* into the palm of her hand and crawled out to the log. She lay the money on top of the log where the shirts had been, placing a pebble on each peso to keep it from blowing away.

Enriquito ran back to the meadow, holding the shirts at arm's length. "Phew!" he squeaked through his pinched nostrils. "What should we do with them?"

Ernestina snapped her fingers. "We'll put some on the pop-up dummies and we can throw the others on the horses as they run by the boulder."

Enriquito drew a diagram on the ground. "I'll drape a shirt on the gate after I close it, and the rest will go on the dummies, but I don't think we should throw them on the horses. They might get too scared and hurt themselves."

"You are the horse expert." Ernestina began mixing up her colors to paint the faces of the dummies.

"Paint the eyes much bigger and darker," Enriquito suggested. "Horses focus on the eyes when they look at a face."

"You are the horse expert," Ernestina mumbled, her

artist's pride slightly ruffled. She squinted down into the painted face even harder and repainted the eyes bigger and darker.

When the coolness of twilight settled into the meadow, it was time to head home.

Ernestina finished spooning the flash powder into the clay pots.

She called out to Enriquito, "All ready over here!"

Enriquito checked his knots one last time and walked to the boulder. *Were they doing the right thing? What if the ponies got too scared and hurt themselves? Maybe they should just leave the ponies alone. They're survivors. They'll go farther up the mountain . . . but then again . . .*

Ernestina called, "I *said*, ready over here!"

Enriquito snapped out of his thoughts. "Ready here!"

They had decided, no turning back now. He did a last-minute check to make sure they had overlooked nothing.

"Now get up on that rock and call them down," Ernestina commanded.

Enriquito climbed up, put his fingers in his mouth, and blew so hard Ernestina thought his eyes might pop out. He blew his silent whistle over and over, waiting and listening as he caught his breath. Finally, from way up on the mountain, came the now familiar sound of muffled hooves on a rocky path, the snap of a twig, a low whinny.

Enriquito leaped off the rock and sprinted to the entrance of the meadow. He backed himself into the bush next to the opening and grabbed the rope that would release the knot. Ernestina ran to the first flash-pot, lay flat on the ground, and covered herself with the tall grass.

Enriquito was surprised to see the stallion already poking his head into the meadow. He would usually take his time reading the wind and carefully looking around to make sure there was no danger before revealing himself and calling in the herd. When the other horses bounded past the stallion into the meadow, Enriquito knew they were losing their fear and becoming careless. Now he had no doubt that their plan was the right thing to do. The ponies had to learn fear again.

The young stallion sensed danger, but he could not hang back now. He flew into the meadow, his tail waving like a flag.

Enriquito pulled hard on the rope, and the whip trees sprang up, blocking the opening. He threw a shirt over one of them and ran, hunched low, over to the flash-pots.

Ernestina was setting off the first smoke plume. It sizzled gold and blue in the pot, and then a thin plume of white smoke rose up and curled delicately. Ernestina thought there was something wrong with the powder, but just as she was about to crawl to it, the white plume grew into a mass of swirling blue-gray smoke. It rose up to twice the height of the rock, a surging, headless human shape, broad at the top and tapering down to the feet.

The horses careened along the border of the meadow, ears swiveling back and forth—spooked by the strange fizz and sizzle of the flash powder. They came around to where the opening used to be. Confused, and frightened by the scent, they veered away at the last moment. With each explosion, they ran in tighter and tighter loops.

Just when it seemed that they couldn't get wilder, Enriquito released the knot that held down the painted dummies. They came whipping up and shook violently in front of the running herd. Some of the shirts flew off the dummies, their sleeves gesturing wildly as they hovered ghostly over the herd.

Ernestina sprinted back to the boulder and climbed up. She saw the stallion running at full speed just below her and the filly running toward him, looking backward at the last flash. There was a dull thud as both horses went down. They skidded across the grass, rolled, and then scrambled back up onto their feet and ran off.

The stallion bit and bumped the panicked horses into the center of the meadow, then pushed them toward the opening.

"Enriquito, open the gate!" Ernestina yelled. She could not stand to see the horses so frightened. Enriquito had just pulled back the whip trees when the herd, trying to funnel through the narrow opening all at once, squeezed by, dangerously close.

Ernestina and Enriquito stood, facing the mountain, breathless. Behind them, the dummies teetered like Sunday-morning Carnival stragglers. Huge clumps of grass and red dirt had been churned up in the once peaceful meadow.

The echoes of thundering hooves and the cries of frightened horses drifted up and were absorbed by the ghostly cloud of smoke hanging above them. An eerie silence fell upon the meadow.

Suddenly, a high-pitched whinny pierced the silence. They followed the sound to the other side of the boulder. The frightened filly was leaning into the boulder, trying to hide.

Enriquito crept closer, picked up an empty burlap bag, and jumped toward the filly. He wrapped the sack around her head and hung on. Ernestina threw her arms around the filly's neck. They blocked her when she tried to jump to the left, then pinned her against the boulder. Her skin rippled and twitched as currents of fear burned through her.

They pushed against her but she did not push back. The filly was not moving!

This frightened Ernestina. "Is she all right? She's not going to die, is she?"

Enriquito huffed back, "No, if horses can't see, they don't move. They could stumble and break a leg."

He stood up and stroked her neck. "Let's see if we can lead her."

Enriquito spoke to the filly in a low voice, just as he had seen his father do with the spooked horses at his uncle's farm. By the time they entered the jungle, her steps had quickened. They climbed along a small trail, following the signs the herd had left as it rumbled up the mountain. Enriquito examined the broken twigs and small branches, hoofprints, even little clumps of horse-hair clinging to the bushes that marked their passing. The jungle thinned out to a field of flat stones, with no soft earth to hold their hoofprints or bushes to catch their hair.

"We've lost the trail," Enriquito said.

"Let her take us the rest of the way," Ernestina whispered. "She's been up and down this way before. Let's see if she knows her way home."

Enriquito loosened his hold on her. "Maybe that will work. But don't take the blindfold off, she might panic and run and she could fall or get lost."

Ernestina was about to start leading her again, when they heard the pounding of hooves and the clatter of rocks just up the hill.

The stallion, raking the air with his hooves, challenged them with an ear-splitting roar.

Ernestina and Enriquito froze.

The filly called back to the stallion.

"He must have been going up and down the trail looking for her," Enriquito whispered.

The stallion turned and disappeared into a grove of ancient trees at the bottom of a cliff.

They ran up to the cliff and searched the ground for hoofprints. Enriquito threw his hands up. "There is no sign of him. Which way do you think he went?"

Ernestina fished a coin from her pocket. "Heads right, tails left?"

"I think we should wait. The stallion might come back," Enriquito said.

"Wait? Are you crazy? It's getting late. What if he doesn't come back?"

"It's the filly you are tossing the coin for. It just doesn't feel right. We should be able to do better than that. Let's look closer for signs."

"Mr. Conscience has spoken," Ernestina said sarcastically.

"What do you mean, *Mr. Conscience*? It's just the right thing to do."

"Enriquito, sometimes you are such a pain. Don't you—"

Before she could finish, Enriquito yelled, "The filly! She's getting away!"

The filly was heading straight for the cliff. When they caught up to her, they gently put their arms around her, but she just kept walking and pulling harder. She would not be held back.

"We are going to crash into the cliff!" Ernestina yelled.

The filly put down her head, as if she were preparing for a collision with the vine-covered wall. She jumped forward, the thick vegetation parted, and they stumbled into a narrow cave.

They lost their footing on the slippery stone floor, and the filly dragged them farther into the dark. She knew this place by feel and smell. Here, the blindfold made no difference.

They bumped around a bend, and then crashed through the green window of foliage at the end of the tunnel.

Ernestina and Enriquito could not hold the filly; she whinnied and leapt away. They went flying off to either side. Ernestina had the blindfold in her hand when she landed. Enriquito lay facedown on the ground.

Ernestina was the first one up. She ran to Enriquito. "*Chico*, are you all right?"

Enriquito didn't answer; he did not move. He was staring past her, over her shoulder.

"Hey, are you okay? What are you looking at?" Ernestina turned around. "Aye, *caramba!*"

A golden shaft of light transformed a waterfall into a shimmering cascade, like jewels tumbling from a treasure chest. A stream rushed over the lush green pastures to feed a lake at the center of the valley. Mango trees and royal palms strolled among the rolling hills to gather around the lake.

Suddenly the valley exploded in a deafening carnival of noise, echoing off the cliffs and making it impossible to pick out the different members of the howling choir.

Then, as suddenly as it began, it stopped. Ernestina followed the ghost of the sound as it spiraled upward and drifted out through the narrow opening.

"Enriquito," she whispered, "this is the most amazing place I've ever been in! I wouldn't be surprised if we were the very first people to set foot in this valley."

"I'll bet you this is where the Paso Finos have been hiding for hundreds of years. See that little path? It was probably made by the horses going down to the lake to drink."

"Let's go!" Ernestina grabbed Enriquito's hand, and they ran down to the large rock jutting out over the water.

From the top of the rock, they had a clear view of the rim of the cliffs overgrown with large trees and vines. The vines looked like dark lace draped across the opening, with little patches of sky shining through.

Enriquito pointed at the top of the cliffs. "Look, both cliffs are exactly the same, no matter which side of the mountain you look at it from. It's like someone cut the mountain, right down the middle, with a big knife. Even if you were flying over it, you probably couldn't see the valley because of all the vines and trees blocking the opening. That's why no one ever found this place."

"When the sun gets down close to the ocean, it won't shine into the valley," Enriquito said as he watched the light climb the cliff walls. "It's going to get dark in here a lot earlier than it is outside."

"How much time do we have?" Ernestina asked as she stared at the sandy bottom of the lake through the crystal-clear water.

"Maybe ten or fifteen minutes," Enriquito said.

The valley was almost completely in shadow now, except for a small spot near the top of the far cliff wall, reaching out for the last rays of the sun. The light was focused there like the beam from a giant magnifying glass, as if the sun were trying to melt the rock to glass. Enriquito tried to look at it, but the brilliant light stung his eyes.

When he closed his eyes, a strange thing happened. A blue spiral with an S-shaped tail floated by, just like when he stared at a lightbulb too long. He could see the blue echo of its shape inside his eyelid. He opened his eyes and looked for the spiral in the shadows on the rocks. When he closed them, it felt as if the little spiral were being pressed onto his forehead. The shape looked so familiar to him. Where had he seen it before?

Then Enriquito heard something splash into the water. Below a bull's-eye of ripples on the surface of the lake, he saw Ernestina swimming for the bottom.

"Ernestina are you crazy?" he yelled.

A big log drifted away from the bank and slowly submerged. Enriquito watched it leisurely paddle toward Ernestina.

"Ernestina, that's not a log!" he yelled. "Aye, *madre mia*! It's huge!"

Enriquito was pumping his arms as if he were pulling on a rope. There was nothing he could do. He could not warn her that the biggest cayman he had ever seen was getting closer with each wag of his tail.

Ernestina had now reached the bottom and was pulling on something that didn't seem to want to let go.

When Ernestina looked up, the cayman was no more than ten feet away. She planted her feet on the sandy bottom and tugged for all she was worth. The smiling cayman unhinged his jaw, preparing for a treat.

Suddenly the thing she was pulling on, a stick about a yard long, came loose, and her arms jerked up over her head. As she lost her grip on the stick, it twirled slowly above her, before disappearing into the cayman's gaping mouth. Ernestina pushed off from the bottom and swam furiously for the surface. The reptile changed course and caught up to her easily. Enriquito could not believe what he was seeing.

Ernestina, knowing she could not outswim the beast, had turned to face her attacker. The cayman rushed in. Ernestina, inside the drawbridge jaws, threw her arms up to try to keep them from closing. Enriquito threw his arms up too, wrapped them around his head, and covered his eyes. He could not bear to see Ernestina, his best friend, chewed to bits, but he could not bear to look away, either. He dropped his arms and opened his eyes.

The cayman snapped his jaws down but they would not close. He opened them again and tried to chew but couldn't. The stick that Ernestina had been pulling on had somehow wedged itself in the reptile's jaws.

Ernestina didn't give the cayman a third chance. She swam out of his mouth and shot up to the surface in a flock of silver bubbles.

Enriquito was jumping up and down, waving his arms. "Ernestina, Ernestina, are you all right?"

"I'm all right, Enriquito." Ernestina's voice quivered.

Enriquito pulled her away from the water. "Ernestina, you're shivering like you were swimming with ice cubes." When she was safely away from the water's edge, he said, "Ernestina! Are you crazy? What were you doing in the water? You didn't tell me you were going in. You weren't even wearing the rope! That thing almost ate you and I couldn't do anything. All I could do was watch."

"I'm sorry, Enriquito. It looked so close, I thought I could just dive in, grab it, and be right back before you knew it." She got Enriquito in a gentle neck lock and rested her cheek on top of his head to calm him down, and to stop herself from shaking.

"Enriquito, your head smells like grass."

Enriquito pulled away. Ernestina had never seen him this scared before.

"We've got to get out of here," he said as he started walking up the path. "I don't want to be here when it gets dark."

Ernestina looked back at the lake. Her teeth were clicking and chattering like little jackhammers.

"*Phew,* that was a close one," she said under her breath—when her jaw stopped rattling. "Did you see what I pulled up?" she called to Enriquito. "It looked like a walking stick with a gold head."

"I didn't see anything except those big teeth!"

"Enriquito, you know that story about Hatuey and the gold his people dumped into a lake?"

"Yeah, I know it. Everyone's been looking for that gold for hundreds of years."

"Enriquito, this could be that lake. That could be the treasure!"

Enriquito stopped. "Ernestina, you just jumped in without saying a word. If you had said something, I could have reminded you of a little detail in the story that you forgot all about."

"What little detail?"

"The little detail about the cayman guarding the treasure. Everybody knows that."

"Oh, yeah, that little detail," Ernestina said lightly.

"Ernestina, that little detail was sixteen feet long and hungry!"

"You are right, Enriquito, you win."

"Our plan worked great, except for one little detail," Enriquito persisted.

"Enriquito, enough about the little detail." Ernestina had her arms crossed, her head tilted, and one eyebrow raised.

Enriquito could see that he had pushed as far as he could. "This detail is about something completely different."

"Oh, we have a new detail?" Ernestina huffed.

"It's about the treasure."

"Enriquito, imagine what it would be like to find the treasure." She could see it clearly. "We'd march right into the town square with the treasure and give it all to the townspeople. Things would be easier for everyone. There would be work in town for our parents and they would not have to go away. The kids would get their parents back and we could all play dominoes on our porches and laugh all night long, like we used to."

"It would be great, but—," Enriquito said glumly.

"But what?" Ernestina didn't really want to know the answer.

Enriquito shook his head. "First of all, there is the

sixteen-foot detail . . . er . . . cayman, and he's not going to let us just swim in and take the treasure."

"We could make a plan. Remember, two heads are better than one. Besides, that cayman's brain is no bigger than my thumbnail. If we can't outsmart him, we are in big trouble." Deep down, Ernestina knew it wouldn't be that easy.

"Think about it, Ernestina. If we did figure out how to get it out, what do you think would happen?" Enriquito's logical brain started clicking. "According to the maps in the town hall, this mountain belongs to *Don* Rigol. If we bring that treasure into town, he will claim it. That's why we have to wait."

"You are right, Enriquito. *Don* Rigol could say that they brought the mountain with them when they came here three hundred years ago, and no one would argue with him. They are all afraid of him. He'll take the treasure and the mountain. Then to top it all off, he'll make us feel like we should be grateful to him for doing it." Ernestina watched the ponies walking down to the lake for their evening drink. "We should have left them alone, this is where they belong."

"It's too late for that, Ernestina. What we have to do now is block up the entrance so that they don't get out. If we don't, someone is bound to find them."

Enriquito wedged the last branch into the barrier, and then Ernestina carefully arranged the vines over the entrance. "There, they won't be able to get past this," Enriquito said, wiping his hands on his shirt.

Ernestina stopped at the mouth of the cave to take a final look. The rocks and trees were glowing with the light they had absorbed during the day. Even the mountain seemed to be floating in the liquid light.

No one, not even Ernestina's mother, could make *ropa vieja* like *Señora* Maruri. It was Ernestina's all-time favorite dish. Skirt steak boiled, shredded into strips, and then cooked in tomato sauce with onions and peppers. It always tickled Ernestina that *ropa vieja*, which means "old clothes," could taste so good.

That night, the usually picky Enriquito ate two helpings. Ernestina broke her own record by eating four heaping plates of it with rice and black beans.

"You two must have been up to some serious playing. I've never seen you eat so much," Enriquito's mother said. Ernestina brought the dishes to the sink; Enriquito washed.

"*Señora*, your food is irresistible. Your *ropa vieja* could turn Mahatma Gandhi into a meat eater. It is the delicious fuel and pure inspiration that drives your exceptional offspring here to achieve at the highest levels of human potential." She rubbed the top of Enriquito's fuzzy head.

"Hey, cut it out!" Enriquito squirmed away from her knuckles.

"If I were to eat at your table every night, there is no telling what great things I would achieve, or how beautiful I would get."

"Ernestina, you are too much." Enriquito's mother laughed sweetly. "You make me want to live to be a very old lady just so that I can see all the great things you and Enriquito will do."

Then she put on her serious face and gave Ernestina's shoulders a little squeeze. "Now, are you going to tell me what's going on?"

Ernestina shot Enriquito a glance and then turned back to *Señora* Maruri. "Going on? Oh, just the usual, you know, school, playing, the usual."

Señora Maruri looked at Enriquito. "Well?"

Ernestina knew they were done for. Enriquito could never hide anything from his mother. Enriquito could not lie.

He said, "You want to tell her or should I?"

"Go ahead," Ernestina said glumly, hoping Enriquito would not tell too much.

Enriquito organized his thoughts, cleared his throat, and, of course, began at the beginning.

He started with the day they found the meadow. He told his mother about the filly, the stallion, and the old mare, and how they were hoping to tame them, little by little, so that they could ride them. He explained how Alysia Rigol-Betancourt had ruined everything.

Ernestina was listening closely, just in case Enriquito let the part about the treasure slip out. Then she jumped in, and with just a little exaggeration, explained how they had made Alysia promise not to tell, then sealed the deal by holding Alysia's grandmother's locket to ensure that she would keep her word. Ernestina fished the locket out of her shirt and held it up.

"May I hold the locket?" *Señora* Maruri asked.

Ernestina released the clasp and handed it to her.

Señora Maruri reached out and gently held it between her thumb and forefinger. A dreamy, faraway look lifted the worry from her face, almost as if the locket were casting a spell on her. She looked off into the distance, through walls and past time.

Enriquito recognized that look; it would come over her sometimes when his father's name was mentioned. He reached up and touched the smooth skin below her chin, just like he had done ever since he was an infant.

Ernestina, who did not like to be left out of anything, tried to squeeze in behind them. She bumped into a large can, where *Señora* Maruri kept her special cookies. It danced along the edge of the counter, then clanged to the floor.

Señora Maruri sat up straight, startled by the loud noise. Ernestina scrambled to gather the cookies. "I am sorry," she said, "I guess I . . ."

Señora Maruri was still sitting with her back as straight as a board, her hands clutching the sides of the table. She was not listening.

"Are you all right? I'm so clumsy. I'm sorry."

Señora Maruri stood up and walked slowly around the table. She stopped by the sink and then turned around, holding the locket in her left hand, cupping her ear with her right, as if she were listening for something.

"Mama, you look as if you've seen a ghost!"

"I feel like I did see a ghost," she replied.

"What is it?" asked Ernestina.

"This locket is the one *Tio* Aurelio made. I'm sure of it." She touched her temples with her fingertips.

"I am a little girl, sitting on my uncle's lap. He is holding the locket in the palm of his hand. My fingers are tracing a shape, no, *he* is drawing the shape with my finger.

"Suddenly, there is a crash behind us! Flowers, soil on the tile floor, he jumps up. I fly off his lap. My mother yells. Uncle Aurelio is really mad. He runs after Juana, the cleaning lady. The front door slams. My mother is picking up the broken flowerpot when he stomps back in, bends down, and writes something in the spilled dirt. She reads it. '*Don* Rigol?'

"I don't think Juana ever came back. I never saw that locket again—until today."

"Are you sure it was this locket?" asked Enriquito.

Señora Maruri carefully inspected the locket. "This is

the one, I can tell by the color of the gold. The only place you'll see that kind of gold is in a museum. That's the gold he used for his jewelry."

The locket was small, oval shaped, like a perfect skipping stone. It had no gems set into it, but it did have a very distinctive pattern of leaves and vines carved into the top and bottom.

Ernestina examined the design closely for the first time. Over time, the pattern in the middle of each face had been rubbed smooth almost to the point of disappearing, but it was clear around the edges—the actual plants that grew in their jungle on the mountain.

Señora Maruri bounced the locket on her hand, testing its weight. "It's so light. It must be hollow," she said.

Enriquito held it, weighed it, and turned it on its side, looking for a seam in the gold. "If it is a locket, it should open, but there are no seams or hinges that I can see." Then he asked, "How come you never told me that story before?"

"Memories are strange, sometimes they hide for a long time. Sometimes, a smell, a face, or a sound is the key that opens the memory trunk. When Ernestina knocked over the can, that noise, your fingers on the locket, that did it. It's strange how fast and clear the pictures came. I think the locket had something to do with that. They say that sometimes things that are made by hand carry the thoughts and wishes of the person who made them."

Ernestina sat up. "Ana, the sculptor, told us about that."

Señora Maruri picked at invisible specks of sugar on the tablecloth. "This world is a mysterious place. People like to think they know how it all works, but no one really does."

"Why didn't your uncle speak?" Ernestina asked *Señora* Maruri. "Was there something wrong with him?"

"No, there was nothing wrong with him. He could speak, but he wouldn't."

"Mama, how come you never talk about your uncle Aurelio? What was he like? If he made that locket, how did Alysia's family end up with it?" Enriquito asked.

"I guess I've been waiting for you to ask that question, because then I would be sure you were old enough for the answer.

"You see, *viejito*, Aurelio's life was full of sadness. No one really knew what made him that way, because he never explained himself. Of course, everyone talked about him. They all had their theories, but I was there, I saw it all as clear as only someone your age can see it."

Señora Maruri smiled sweetly at her son. Then she got up and lit a burner on the stove to heat up some coffee. She reached into the cupboard, took out three glasses and poured cold lemonade into two of them. Then she opened the jar of *guayava* shells floating in sugary syrup she had made that afternoon. When her coffee was ready, she poured two fingers of it into her glass and set out the dishes and little spoons.

When everything was laid out just right, *Señora* Maruri hung her apron on the back of the chair, smoothed the tablecloth once more, and began.

"It all starts with my grandfather, your great-grandfather, Ricardo, the goldsmith. He came here from Spain as a young man to work for his uncle, who had a jewelry shop in Havana. They say that he had a special feel for the work, and by the time his uncle died, Ricardo was already known as the best goldsmith on the island. He moved his shop to this town and built his house high up on the hill. People would come from as far away as Oriente Province to buy his jewelry.

"When Aurelio was born, Ricardo placed his crib in the workshop so that he could start teaching him right away. He wanted his son to follow in his footsteps.

"In the evening, Ricardo and Aurelio would sit on the veranda of the house and look out over the bay. *Señor* Luz, *el Viejo*'s father, would come up every night. They would talk and play dominoes—enjoy the breeze.

"My grandfather, Ricardo, was very interested in the history of Cuba, the Caribbean, and gold. You see, when Cuba was the most important colony of the Spanish Empire, ships from all the other colonies would stop in Havana before sailing across the Atlantic to Spain. They came to Havana filled with Aztec and Incan gold objects. They would melt these beautiful cups, crowns, and other things down into ingots. Then the galleons, heavy with gold, would form a convoy and be escorted back to Spain."

Enriquito interrupted, "Why did they need to be escorted back to Spain? Couldn't they find their way back by themselves?"

Señora Maruri smiled. "It's as simple as planting beans, Enriquito. First, you get some gold. Then you add water, and you'll sprout pirates and privateers. The Spaniards took the gold from the natives. Then the pirates stole the gold from the Spaniards.

"The pirates knew that, if they were found with as much as one single button stolen from the royal ships, they would be hanged immediately. No trial, no lawyers. Their game was to rob, pillage, and then get rid of the loot as quickly as possible. The pirates became experts at hiding things. This coast was perfect for the game because of all the little islands, inlets, and jungles.

"When my grandfather was a young man, someone actually found a small treasure chest buried by pirates. From that day on, everybody in town became a treasure hunter. It was like a hobby. Every Saturday, you would see groups of grown men going off to dig holes in the middle of nowhere. They usually had a real 'treasure map,' which they bought from the 'treasure experts' who came to town right after the first treasure was found. These maps were all fake, and the men probably knew it, but they wanted to believe in their great adventure, so they didn't ask too many questions.

"My grandfather caught the treasure fever too. He read every book he could get his hands on. He was fascinated by the tale of Hatuey's gold. Many people thought it was just a myth, but Ricardo was convinced that it really happened. Unlike the others, he knew what he was looking for. His friend and partner, *Señor* Luz, knew the jungle better than anyone in the area. They made a pretty good team. They never told anyone what they were up to, but people put two and two together.

"On the day that Ricardo, *Señor* Luz, and Aurelio climbed up the mountain, everyone knew, including the Rigols, that it wasn't pirates' treasure they were looking for.

"We stayed up all night waiting. When they weren't back the next morning, some of their friends set off to look for them. Four days later, Aurelio came back, alone."

Señora Maruri took a loud sip of coffee. "Ay, it's so bitter and cold." Her little spoon found the sugar bowl. Halfway back to the cup, it stopped and hovered in midair. *Señora* Maruri was looking through the walls again.

"I can see Aurelio, exhausted, unsure, at the courtyard gate. His clothes are wet and torn. We ask about his father and *Señor* Luz. He shivers and shakes, covers his head with his hands, and cries. He tries to talk but his words come out all jumbled, like a dropped puzzle.

"We finally get him into his bedroom. All night long, he cries. His nightmares must be terrifying. Every morning, we set a place for him, but he never comes back to the table. He never rejoins our world.

"At night we hear him padding around the house like a sleepwalker, and then the squeak of hinges on the door of the workshop. This is where he had spent many happy hours with his father, learning the language of the tools and the secrets of the gold. It made him feel better to be there, closer to his father.

"One morning we find a piece of jewelry on the table, where my grandfather used to sit. It looks exactly like the things he used to make. Two or three times a month, a new piece appears at the head of the table.

"Of course, everyone is saying that it is the ghost of Ricardo who is back at work in his shop.

"The word spreads about the 'miraculous' appearance of the jewelry; people start coming from as far away as Havana to buy it. There is nothing like a good piece of gold with a mysterious history!

"Gradually, he starts using the local flowers and vines that grow on the mountain in his patterns and decorations. Whether he knows it or not, his unique designs are supporting the whole family.

"Eventually, we discover that it is Aurelio who is making the jewelry. The word gets around, but it doesn't seem to bother the buyers. To the contrary, it's an interesting twist to the story, and it makes it even more desirable.

"People come from all over to meet him, to beg him to make special things for them. Most of the time, he slams the shutters in his room that he built to keep them, and the sun, out, and then goes back to sleep.

"Still, he walks around the house every night. It's like living with a ghost, but I guess you get used to anything.

"Then"—*Señora* Maruri taps her temple—"I'm almost sure it was a little after Juana left, something very strange happens. In the middle of the night, I hear doors slamming, birds screeching in their cages. Everyone is in the courtyard, running around in their long cotton nightgowns. It looks like a ghost convention that got out of hand. They are all jumping around Aurelio, asking him what happened. I can remember thinking, Now he's going to speak, but he doesn't say a word. He picks up a burlap bag, I hear metal clanging and, as he walks past me, he looks at me with his sad eyes. He speaks to me for the first and last time. He says, 'The locket.' His voice is raspy.

"I never saw that locket again—until today."

Señora Maruri glanced up at the clock. "Ay, *mira la hora*! How did it get this late? That's all for tonight."

"Wait, Mama," Enriquito said. "If Aurelio kept making gold jewelry, why didn't he run out of gold? Did you ever find out what was in the sack?"

Ernestina sat up and added, "I bet Aurelio had his

reasons for suspecting that the Rigols were spying on him. My father's favorite joke is, 'Where there is gold, there is a Rigol.'"

"Enough now. Wash up, go to sleep, both of you." *Señora* Maruri sounded very stern.

"Mama, I bet he found Hatuey's gold up in the mountain."

Ernestina pinched Enriquito hard under the table, and *Señora* Maruri shot up from her chair. Ernestina thought she had pinched the wrong leg.

"That's it! This book is closed!" *Señora* Maruri said.

"But why?" Enriquito pleaded.

Ernestina had never seen her so upset.

"I'll tell you why. That gold brought nothing but sadness to the house where I grew up. I will not allow that curse into my house."

Señora Maruri moved around the kitchen like an efficient little machine, rattling dishes, closing the cabinet doors just a little too hard. Ernestina tried to help, but *Señora* Maruri took the glasses away from her. She cupped Ernestina's face in her hands and said, "You must give the locket back to Alysia. You have no idea how much trouble it could bring down on our heads."

A thousand questions kept Enriquito awake. He reached for the locket on the night table—holding it made him feel calmer. It was warm, alive like the clay heart he held at Ana's studio. Maybe it was Hatuey's heart, or Aurelio's, he could feel beating, faintly, inside the old gold.

Enriquito's eyelids grew heavy. He tumbled backward into a warm sea of dreams.

As usual, Enriquito woke up without an alarm clock. Sitting on the edge of the bed, he watched the white curtain billow like a sail, empty, then flatten against the screen.

His mother was in the kitchen, the water flowing.

The water is flowing, a waterfall, the dream.

The cliff above the waterfall is on fire. Flames leap into the sky, blazing spirals reach for the sun. His finger is tracing a shape over and over on the locket's smooth face. Then it opens. A small tube of paper tied with a red thread begins to unravel, then the voice: "It's gone."

Enriquito was staring at the billowing curtain when his mother came in.

"Good morning, Enriquito." She leaned over him. "What are you looking at?"

Enriquito stood up suddenly.

"Enriquito, what's going on?"

Enriquito jumped into his shorts and grabbed his stinky sneakers from the windowsill. He was about to run out of the room with yesterday's T-shirt in his hand.

"Enriquito, stop right this minute! What is the matter with you?"

Enriquito, twisting and spinning, was trying to get out of his mother's grasp. "Mama, Mama, let me go, I have to get to Ernestina. I can't let her return the locket. There is something inside."

"Enriquito, she has to return it. I told her to return it."

"Please, Mama, it's our last chance to find out!" He jerked in the opposite direction and she lost her grip.

He was in midair over the front porch steps when he heard his mother screaming, "Enriquito!"

He jumped over the gate and ran down the road, leaving little puffs of dust floating above the sand as if his sneakers were on fire.

Ernestina's fancy girls' school was three miles from their house. Enriquito didn't slow down until he could see the school at the top of the hill. As he ran up to the building, he searched for a side door. Ernestina had told him that there was a guard at the front doors, provided, of course, by *Don* Rigol to keep "the little angels" safe, especially his "little angel," Alysia.

He was drenched in sweat, trying to catch his breath. Stopping Ernestina from handing back the locket was the only thing he was thinking about when he left the house. He had no idea how he was going to do that. He had no plan.

What would Ernestina do?

He tried to grab the knob, but his hands were sweaty and he could not get a good grip. He wrapped his T-shirt around the knob. Luckily, it was unlocked. He took a deep breath and swung the door open.

He found himself in the middle of a long hallway. There were girls everywhere, fancy girls who smelled like soap and wore beautiful combs in their hair.

Little fingers of fear tapped along every nerve in his body. He was stuck to the wall like a fly to sticky tape. When he realized it was the sweat on his back that made him stick, he smiled to himself and peeled himself off.

He swung the door open and plunged into a sea of starched cotton shirts, suffocating hair, and nauseating perfume. He was running and weaving as fast as he could through the crowd. A high-pitched screech came scratching up behind him and almost knocked him down.

He finally spotted her just fifteen feet away. She was facing Alysia, about to hand her something.

Enriquito leaped into the air. "Ernestina!"

Flying, in slow motion, through the swirling, jerking bodies, he could make out the girls' expressions as they cried out, but there was no sound. He grasped the locket and tore it out of Ernestina's hand.

Sound and speed returned as he hit the marble floor with a thud and slid on his stomach toward an exit. He got up and scampered to the door, like a mouse frantic for his hole.

Just as he reached for the doorknob, something

grabbed him by the collar. He began to rise, high above the gathering crowd. Hovering near the ceiling, he came eye to eye with the principal of the school.

Padre Casas was not at all amused. "Well, well, what do we have here?" The principal held him at arm's length as if he were a strange bug.

Ernestina had just run up behind them as the *padre* swung Enriquito toward the principal's office. When they collided, Enriquito threw his arms and legs around Ernestina, clinging onto her like a tick. The priest tried to pull him away, but Enriquito would not let go. When Padre Casas turned to open the door, Enriquito slipped the locket inside Ernestina's book bag. He let go of Ernestina just as the principal opened the door to drag them both into his office. Enriquito flew into the room, slid across the priest's desk, spilled a bottle of black ink on the red leather blotter, bumped into the wall, and dropped behind the desk.

Ernestina put down her bag just outside the office and rushed over to the far side of the desk. "*Loco*, what are you doing here?"

Alysia charged into the room. "Arrest this little beast! He has stolen my priceless locket. I was just showing it to this girl and he grabbed it!"

Enriquito slid farther under the desk.

Alysia shot Ernestina a triumphant look. She had just told a huge lie, but there was nothing Ernestina could say. How could she explain Alysia's locket without giving the ponies away?

The priest stepped around the desk. "Who are you?"

A determined voice rose through the desk. "I'm Enriquito Maruri."

"Enriquito Maruri, I want you to give *Señorita* Rigol her locket back," the priest said in his most patient voice.

"I don't have her locket," Enriquito answered.

"He's a liar. He grabbed it right out of my hands!" Alysia yelled.

"Young man, if you don't return the locket, I will have to search you personally," the priest threatened.

"I don't have it. If I don't have it, I can't return it, can I? So if you want to search me, go ahead!" Enriquito, usually respectful to adults and other large creatures, sounded very angry.

He threw his arms up and turned away from the *padre*. For a moment, he faced Ernestina and winked at her, then turned slowly toward Alysia and stuck out his tongue at her. Alysia jumped back, disgusted, as if she had just seen a large worm crawl out of his mouth. The priest ordered him to stop turning so he could search him. He patted him up and down, but he found nothing. Enriquito kept his arms up, daring him to search him again.

Ernestina was as puzzled as Alysia.

Alysia eyed Ernestina suspiciously. "Search Ernestina,"

Alysia commanded. "They are best friends. I'll bet he slipped it to her."

Ernestina shrugged her shoulders. The priest picked up the phone and called for a nun. As they waited, Ernestina tried to act cool and innocent.

"I don't know how you could say that we are best friends. He is just a kid, besides everyone knows that he is a little ... well, you know ..." Ernestina twirled her index finger in a circle at her right temple, the universal *loco* sign. Enriquito peeked over the desk, eyebrows arched like question marks.

Sister Theresa entered the principal's office without knocking. She cleared her throat and interrupted Ernestina. "Well, what mischief has our little Ernestina gotten into?"

"Sister, a piece of jewelry has been stolen. I need you to search Ernestina," the principal said.

Sister Theresa grabbed Ernestina's arm and led her into the bathroom.

Alysia called the guard over. Rodolfo had been waiting outside the room, worrying that *Don* Rigol was going to take away his job because he wasn't paying attention when Enriquito ran in. Alysia ordered him to call her father.

The *padre* said, "I think we should wait. *Don* Rigol is a very busy man. I will call him when we have something to tell him."

Alysia grabbed the guard's thin red tie and spoke loudly into his ear so that not only he, but also the priest could hear. "You will call right now." The guard knew it was *Don* Rigol who signed his paycheck, not the *padre*, so he went off to make the call.

Enriquito was still peeking over the desk when Sister Theresa pushed Ernestina back into the room. "I found nothing."

Alysia was livid. "What do you mean, you found nothing? How could that locket just disappear? He took it right out of my hands." She glared at Enriquito. "You little rat! How dare you even think that you could take something that belongs to me!"

Enriquito stood up and said in his coolest tone, "Maybe I don't think it belongs to you."

Just then the guard returned and whispered to Alysia that her father and the judge were on their way.

"We will wait until my father gets here. He'll know how to deal with you," Alysia said, gloating.

Enriquito stared at Ernestina with no expression on his face. He raised his eyebrow just a fraction of a centimeter as his eyes shot to the bottom of the door. Ernestina got the message: the book bag, by the door.

The bell rang for class. Ernestina knew this might be her only chance to escape with her bag before they realized the obvious.

"Alysia, I'm sure you will find your locket. Please be

patient with him." She nodded toward Enriquito. "I think he has temporarily lost his marbles." Then she asked the *padre* if she could go on to her next exam. The *padre* thought about it for a moment and then said, "By all means, my child, go. If we need to talk to you, we will call you."

Ernestina could tell that Enriquito was scared but trying not to show it. His eyebrows were arched like the roof of a house; she thought she saw his lower lip quiver.

Ernestina slipped through the door, closed it, nonchalantly grabbed her book bag, and walked down the hall.

Soon, Alysia would tick off the possibilities, realize the obvious, and come for her bag. There was no time to waste.

When she was safely around the corner, she reached deep into the bag and there it was, the locket, wedged between her notebook and a half-eaten empanada. She kept her hand and the locket deep in the bag while she looked for a place to hide it.

Up ahead, a group of girls was talking in front of the school trophy case. She squeezed in between them and the trophies, turned toward the wall, then slipped the locket into a large cup with handles shaped like wings.

Right before she got to her classroom, she felt something tugging at her book bag. Sister Theresa had her arm, up to her elbow, in Ernestina's bag, rummaging furiously through her things.

"I've been instructed to search this," she declared.

Ernestina let go of the bag. "Help yourself."

Sister Theresa pulled the bag from Ernestina's shoulder, dumped everything out on a table, and began to pick through her things. When she finished, Ernestina said, "Sister, I don't have the locket."

"My dear, I knew you were a sneaky one from the moment I laid my eyes on you. In my book, you'll always be guilty." She whirled around and headed back to the office.

Don Rigol, sitting in the principal's leather chair, was listening intently as Padre Casas recounted the details of the crime. When the nun came in, he held up his hand, silenced the priest, then signaled for her to speak.

"*Don* Rigol, I found nothing on the girl, but I am positive she had something to do with this," Sister Theresa sniveled.

Don Rigol turned to Enriquito. He spoke slowly and deliberately.

"This is not an ordinary theft. The locket is a very important family heirloom, immensely valuable. For this reason, the criminal will not be treated as, say, a pickpocket or a cat burglar. No, this crime is more serious than that. You can be assured that the penalties will be very, very severe. Isn't that right, Judge?"

The judge was not paying attention. He was busy trying to match names to faces on a wall of graduation pictures.

Don Rigol impatiently repeated, "Judge! Would you agree that the penalties would be very, very severe?"

"Very, very severe, er . . . Yes, most severe," the judge, as usual, parroted *Don* Rigol.

Don Rigol turned back to Enriquito. "It would be a tragedy to have to lock up someone as young as yourself. Tell us what you did with the locket, and the judge might show pity on you." Enriquito crossed his arms and stuck out his lower lip. He was not about to give in.

"Judge, tell our stubborn little criminal how much easier things will go for him if he admits he is wrong. . . . Judge!"

The judge was staring into the sea of hopeful graduates, marveling over their changing hairstyles. "Fascinating, how their hairstyles change so gradually. I'll bet they didn't even notice the change."

"Yes, very fascinating, Your Honor, and I am sure you will find it equally fascinating just how quickly one's job title can change."

The judge understood. "This is a clear case of grand theft, breaking and entering, trespassing, and scaring innocent schoolchildren. Yes, very, very serious. But, of course, if the stolen item is returned, I would take that into consideration when I decide the punishment."

Enriquito sank behind the desk, rested his chin on its cool polished edge, and stared at the judge. He wondered if he remembered.

A few years ago, he and Ernestina had pulled the judge out of the bay after he fell off the Rigols' yacht. The deck was crowded with ladies and gentlemen dressed in white, holding drinks. Ernestina called out, "Man overboard!" But no one turned around.

Later on, when they told *el Viejo* about the incident, he laughed. He had met the judge when he worked on the crew of that yacht. One of the crewmembers told him that the man had gone off to school in Havana to study law, but he was more interested in parties than books. When his father realized this, he made a very generous donation to the university and the son received his law degree. They shipped him back home and *Don* Rigol made him a judge.

Enriquito popped up like a marionette. "How come your cousin is the judge?"

Anger flashed across *Don* Rigol's face. Then he smiled and said dismissively, "Just one of those coincidences." Then the anger returned. "Now, tell me where the locket is before I lose my patience."

Enriquito persisted. "How come you ended up with the locket?"

Don Rigol tightened his mouth and growled through his teeth, "What do you mean?"

Enriquito looked straight at *Don* Rigol. "I mean that my mother's uncle Aurelio made that locket for her, then it was stolen right out of his workshop by your greasy thief."

Sister Theresa leaned over the desk and tried to give Enriquito one of her painful ear pulls, but he saw it coming and ducked.

"Why, you insolent little peasant, how dare you speak to *Don* Rigol that way!"

"I am just telling the truth," Enriquito shot back.

For a moment, *Don* Rigol looked startled, but then he said, "I am afraid your questions will remain unanswered. I've had enough of this little game."

He rubbed his hands together and said to the guard, "Rodolfo, you will take him to the jail cell in the courthouse. He will be your responsibility until we decide what to do with him."

Enriquito sat on the edge of the cot, lost in thought. Outside, the wind ruffled the green jungle canopy to silver as clouds sailed across an impossibly blue sky. Twin columns of brown smoke rose from the lower portion of the mountain.

"It's not right," Enriquito mumbled to himself. "That locket belongs around Mama's neck, not Alysia's."

With the blue mountain as his witness, Enriquito vowed he would not give up the locket. No matter what happened, this time, the Rigols were not going to win.

He was not going to sit and wait while they decided

his fate. He would turn his brain into a key and think his way out.

The walls of the jail cell were made of brick. The door was split in the middle. The bottom half was solid wood, and the top was made of iron bars. The same bars enclosed the window on the back wall. Enriquito figured that at one time this had been a mailroom, because of the wooden cubbyholes that lined two of the walls. Now he began measuring everything he could get his hands on. He knew that from the tip of his thumb to the tip of his little finger was six inches. The window was twenty-eight inches wide and thirty-two inches tall. He walked his hand over the terra-cotta floor tiles. They were twelve-inch squares. The door was thirty inches across.

He was walking across the cell, counting footsteps, when he heard Rodolfo's gravelly voice in the other room and his mother calling, "En-ri-qui-to, Enriquito, are you here?" His heart sank. Her voice reminded him—now it was very real—they might take him away from his mother. What would she do without him? He had promised his father that he would always take care of her.

"Mama! Mama! I'm here, in the back!" he called as tears bloomed in his eyes.

"I'm coming!" his mother yelled. "You better get out of my way, you big oaf, or I swear by my grandmother's bones you will be wearing these black beans and rice on your head."

Señora Maruri came charging around the corner, followed by Rodolfo.

"Enriquito, what happened?" *Señora* Maruri cried out.

"I am so sorry, Mama. I couldn't let them get the locket back. It doesn't belong to them."

"The minute I saw that locket again, I knew there would be trouble." *Señora* Maruri pulled out her handkerchief and wiped a tear from Enriquito's eye.

"Mama, don't worry, we are right and they are wrong, and like you always say, right always wins."

"Enriquito, you don't know the Rigols. They can get really mean." *Señora* Maruri pleaded, "Please, tell them where the locket is!"

"I can't, Mama. I just can't." Enriquito tried to sound brave, but a little quiver in his voice gave him away.

Rodolfo came in and announced that he had been instructed to allow only very brief visits.

Señora Maruri moaned, "He's my son."

"I know. I am sorry." Rodolfo was not completely heartless.

Then *Señora* Maruri said softly, "You must have been someone's *niño* at one time. You must have had a mother who loved you?"

Two or three different emotions chased each other

around Rodolfo's face as he gently led *Señora* Maruri out of the cell.

That night, Enriquito dreamed he was drifting out to sea in a boat without oars.

The next morning, Ernestina came in early with breakfast. Enriquito was measuring the opening between the iron bars of the windows with a thread that he had carefully pulled out of the waistband of his shorts.

"Hey, jailbird," Ernestina called out. "You look busy. What are you doing?"

"Hi, Ernestina. I was just taking some measurements."

"Are you planning on decorating?" Ernestina set down the basket of food that *Señora* Maruri had made for him. "Your mama sends her love. She took the early bus to Havana to try to get help. She told me not to tell you, but she is really worried about you."

Ernestina opened the basket, pulled out a banana, and then whispered, "Enriquito, what got into you, flying into school like that? I thought you had gone completely *loco*."

Enriquito touched her hand and whispered, "Did you find it?"

Ernestina nodded and said loudly, "Have some of that fresh mango juice. It's right there, at the bottom of the basket."

Enriquito put his hand into the basket and found a small bundle. His penknife, watch, pencil, paper, and a ball of string, all wrapped in rubber bands. This was the stuff he usually carried around in his pockets. Without it, nothing seemed possible. Now, he could think and plan.

He smiled and winked at Ernestina and said, "Mmmm. Tell Mama the juice was just what I needed." Then he whispered, "Can you bring it?"

"I'll tell her to make you some more," Ernestina said cheerfully. Then she leaned closer to Enriquito. "That's not a good idea. If they catch you with it, they'll send you away. *Don* Rigol is not fooling around."

Enriquito insisted. "You have to bring it."

Ernestina stared at her hands. "Enriquito, I am sorry you have to be here. I would change places with you if I could."

He felt something inside start to give, like the walls of the sandcastles they built too close to the waves. Something was crumbling, but he couldn't let it fall. He jumped up, tucked the bundle under the mattress, and said, "Ernestina, this time they are not going to win."

Rodolfo came walking around the corner to announce the end of the visit. Ernestina got up, winked at Enriquito, and said to Rodolfo, "What do you mean, it's over? I just got here."

"Sorry, *niñita*. I don't make the rules, I just follow them."

Before Enriquito could stop her, Ernestina launched into Rodolfo. "Who are you calling *niñita*? I can climb a tree like a lizard, swim like a shark, run like a deer!"

Enriquito grabbed the food basket and began to push her out of the cell.

Ernestina continued as she was led out into the hall. "I can outrun, outwrestle, outthink, and outtalk any boy my age. And you call me a *'little girl'*?"

Rodolfo waited patiently for her to finish. "Good day, *Señorita* Ernestina. I look forward to your next visit."

Enriquito heard Ernestina laugh. "I am sure you do, Rodolfo. I'll be back with dinner to relieve your boredom."

Rodolfo returned to Enriquito's cell and stuck his big head in. "That Ernestina is something else. She is going to be a terror when she grows up."

"We're best friends and—"

Rodolfo interrupted him. "How come you have a girl for a best friend?"

Enriquito thought about it for a second. "I don't know. I never thought of Ernestina like that."

"You are lucky to have a friend like her and a good family to take care of you," Rodolfo said on the way out. "*Don* Rigol doesn't like to feed jailbirds."

In the evening, Ernestina returned with Enriquito's dinner. Rodolfo got up from his desk, bowed, and then ceremoniously announced, "*Señorita* Ernestina the Great has returned!"

Ernestina strolled in like a queen and smiled. "It is so very nice to see you. Rodolfo, please stand up, I wouldn't want you to hurt your back."

Rodolfo smiled. "You have five minutes. I hope you enjoy your visit."

Ernestina sat down next to Enriquito on the cot and got right down to business. "Enriquito, they're clearing the jungle all the way to the top of the mountain."

Enriquito glanced at the window. "I can see that." He had been watching the clearing of the green canopy, climbing higher up the mountain, closer to the secret valley.

"The real bad news is that they found the entrance to the valley."

"What have they done with the ponies?"

"They drove them down to the Rigols' place," Ernestina said.

Enriquito paced from the door to the window. "Those ponies belong on the mountain. They need to be wild. We have to come up with a plan, we have to do something!"

Rodolfo grunted in the front room, signaling that the visit was coming to an end. Enriquito whispered, "Did you bring what I asked for?"

"Yes, but be careful. That's the only thing that's keeping them from sending you away." Ernestina reached into the dinner basket, cupped the locket in her hand, and tucked it under the pillow.

"Out! All visitors out of the building," boomed the bored Rodolfo.

The mountain cut a blue silhouette against the violet sky. A dog barked up in the hills. Soon the lights of the square would be turned on, and families would come to take their evening stroll.

"You know, I am a prisoner too. I'll be in jail until they decide what they are going to do with you," Rodolfo complained. "If I were you, I would give them what they want. I've heard them talking. If you don't cooperate, they'll have a trial and send you away."

"A trial for me?"

"Yes, for you. You have something the Rigols want. One way or the other, they always get what they want."

Families and couples had begun to trickle into the square. Enriquito watched them restlessly swirling about in little groups.

"Look, down there, you see those people? They are all talking about you."

"They are talking about me?"

"You, the clearing of the mountain, and the ponies. They don't like what's going on, and they are getting mad." He looked around, leaned in a little closer, and whispered, "Everyone knows you stood up to the Rigols, and it just might inspire others to actually do something. That would *not* be good—the Rigols don't like it when people get in their way." Rodolfo lit a match and held it close to Enriquito's nose. "You're the match in their dry sugarcane." Then he blew out the match.

As Rodolfo walked out of the cell, he warned Enriquito, "Remember, *chico*, one way or the other, they always get what they want."

Enriquito stood at the window, watching as the little groups turned into a large, noisy crowd that filled the square.

A woman who looked like Ana climbed up on the bandstand. The crowd roared. It sounded like a large angry animal was trapped in the square. Enriquito could not hear a word she was saying.

Suddenly, the lights went out. A dark blanket fell over the square, and the crowd was paralyzed. Just like the blindfolded filly, if they could not see, they wouldn't move. The circle of darkness grew as the streetlights, and finally all the houses of the town, went dark.

Then somebody shouted, "Run! Run for your life!"

The crowd, like a sleeper rudely awakened, bumped into lampposts, buildings, and each other, then they scattered. All that remained were the echoes of their footsteps and little pieces of paper blowing lonely in the evening breeze.

Enriquito was sure that somewhere, *Don* Rigol had his hand on a big light switch, and he was laughing.

Enriquito waited in the dark until he heard loud snores coming from the room next door.

He reached under the pillow, found the locket, and cupped it against his face. It felt warm, a certain kind of warm, like the warmth of his mother's hand.

Enriquito started to drift off.

Spilled water flowing over the edge of a table.

A blazing waterfall tumbling in slow motion into a lake. The moon-sized magnifying glass focuses its beam on the top of the cliff, glowing rocks melt. A spiral with a curving tail hovers over his hand, his fingertips read the etched vines as they disappear at the center of the locket. Then the little spiral settles into its blank, glowing heart.

Was he dreaming or awake? He felt something click in his hand. The sigh of a golden hinge threaded softly into his ear. Like a flower slowly unfolding, the locket opened.

In the center of the locket lay a small roll of paper tied with a crimson thread. He untied the knot, and the paper, as thin as the skin of an onion, unrolled by itself to welcome the kiss of the moonlight.

Words, in a brown, masculine script, marched across the parchment and lifted off.

They swirled around his head like a banner, speaking

to him in a strangely familiar voice. He was certain the voice belonged to the mysterious Aurelio.

My destiny, and this locket, were both fashioned from the gold Hatuey drowned.

This wondrous metal, my only companion, heard the words I could speak to no one else. In return, it revealed its secrets to me. With this knowledge, I have crafted this vessel that will open only for you of my blood. You have seen the shining key. You will know my secret.

It was a proud day when I accompanied my father and Señor Luz into the mountains to search for treasure.

We passed through a cave into a beautiful valley that no Spaniard had ever seen. In the center of this valley, there was a lake surrounded by a small prairie. We were sure this was the lake mentioned in the old story of Hatuey's gold. Standing on a large rock that rose above the water, we could see many shining objects lying on a mound at the bottom of the crystal-clear lake.

Señor Luz swam to the bottom and brought back a child's bracelet. When he dived in again, a monstrously large cayman appeared out of nowhere and swam straight for him.

My father jumped in to try and save him.

The cayman spun like a green whirlpool with his disoriented victims in his great jaws. He dragged my father and Señor Luz down to the deep end of the lake.

For three days, I ran along the shore calling out their names. Finally, I gave up, and somehow found my way home.

The memory of those terrifying events frightened my words away. I lost count of the days, but my silence served me well. I realized that if I told my story, I would have to reveal the location of the valley. I knew that the Rigols would then lay claim to Hatuey's gold, and my father and Señor Luz would have died in vain.

I never removed the treasure from the lake, knowing that there was no safer place for it.

I did return to the lake many times to gather gold for my work. In order to do this, I made a collar and a long chain that I attached to a sturdy spike driven into the ground. The chain and collar are buried near the stake.

My enemy, the cayman, became my ally. The frequently dozing monster would be collared and secured by the chain while I brought up the gold. Then, by pulling the cord attached to the latch, I would release him again to guard the gold.

The Tainos could see into the dark hearts of

*those who worship gold as their god. They under-
stood that they would stop at nothing to get it.
These people are still with us today, and I have no
doubt that they will be with us tomorrow.*

*You, of my blood, with a true heart, must
redeem the treasure in the service of something
noble and good.*

This is the true history of Aurelio Maruri.

Enriquito, aware of an intense light shining down on him,
felt himself shaking—no— being shaken. His eyes were
open and someone was speaking to him. "Aurelio? Why
are you shaking me? Why are you laughing?"

"Well, well, what do we have here? Could this be the
famous locket everyone has been looking for?" Rodolfo
shook Enriquito again. "*Oye, chico,* wake up, I think your
little goose is cooked."

Enriquito climbed out of his dream to find Rodolfo's
face, too close. He could smell the morning coffee on his
breath. The locket swung like a pendulum in front of him.
He tried to grab it, but it was just out of reach.

"It's too late for that. I've been watching and waiting.
I knew you were up to something. You were waiting for
me to go to sleep, but I was waiting for you." He made
loud snoring sounds and began to laugh. "Instead, you

are the one who fell asleep. You made it too easy. You can't outsmart Rodolfo, no sir."

Enriquito was confused. Had he been dreaming or awake all night? Had he actually opened the locket and heard Aurelio's story? He sat up on the cot and stared past Rodolfo as he boasted and strutted around the cell. Enriquito tried to organize his thoughts, to separate what he knew was real from what he thought he had dreamed.

The Rigols had the locket, the ponies, and the mountain. They would probably send him away as a thief, never to see his mother or Ernestina again, never to sail *L'il Havana* or roam the mountain.

There was only one thing he could do. He needed to push those feelings back, to stay calm. The mysterious images of the dream gave him hope. Maybe the dream was like the word puzzles he and Ernestina did on rainy days. Maybe if he could unscramble the images and put them in order, the message would reveal itself to him.

"I can't wait to see *Don* Rigol's face when I hand him the locket," Rodolfo gushed. "He better grease my palm with a big reward."

Enriquito looked up at Rodolfo. Something started to spin. "Did you say *grease?*" Enriquito asked carefully.

"Yeah, *grease*, as in 'grease my palm'—a reward—for catching you with this necklace." Rodolfo did not see the little light burning inside of Enriquito's head as he taunted him with the dangling locket.

"Yeah, right, grease," Enriquito repeated. He glanced past Rodolfo at the iron bars on the window. His hand searched his pocket for the little piece of thread he had pulled off his shorts, the thread he had used to compare the opening between the bars to the size of his head. He found the string balled up at the bottom of his pocket. The little knots he made to record his measurements were still there.

With his pencil and paper, he could think, make a plan.

He would slip a note to Ernestina in the breakfast basket.

Ernestina stood at the desk that Rodolfo had set up by the front door. He watched closely as she opened the dinner basket and took out each item. She placed two identical jars on the desk, opened one, and said, "Pudding."

Rodolfo dipped his finger into the dark brown goo, then licked it.

"Hmmm, chocolate. My favorite flavor."

"Rodolfo, do you always stick your fat finger in other people's desserts?" Ernestina took a spoon out of the basket and handed it to Rodolfo.

"Here, you might as well finish it, I brought two."

As he dug into the pudding, she put the other jar back

in the basket and walked into the cell.

"Make sure you eat every bit of that dinner, Enriquito. You know how your mother worries when you don't eat. You even have chocolate pudding for dessert."

Enriquito looked up calmly. Ernestina knew how much he hated chocolate pudding. He looked toward the other room and spoke softly, "There is going to be a full moon tonight, but the clouds will be heavy and low."

Ernestina looked into Enriquito's eyes and nodded slowly. She understood.

Just then Rodolfo burst into the room and announced that the visit was over. He ushered Ernestina out without any of the usual pleasantries, leaving Enriquito to eat his dinner all alone.

Enriquito finished and put everything back into the basket. Later on, when Rodolfo came back for the basket and for his final search of the day, he noticed the little jar sitting on the windowsill.

"If you are not going to eat the pudding, can I have it?"

"No, I'm saving that for later," Enriquito answered.

Rodolfo was disappointed.

"You can have my tea. My mother makes it from the herbs in our garden. She puts in lots of the good honey from the mountain." Enriquito knew Rodolfo could not resist anything sweet. Rodolfo took the tea, made a quick inspection of the cell, and left. About an hour later, Enriquito heard growling, gurgling, and then whistling coming from the front room. Rodolfo had to be sound asleep; no human could make a noise like that on purpose. The tea Rodolfo drank was the same stuff Enriquito's mother gave him when he had a fever. It always knocked him out. It was brewed from a special plant that an old lady collected on the mountain and sold in town. Knowing Ernestina, she had probably made it strong enough to put two Rodolfos to sleep.

Enriquito looked out the window. A curtain of dark clouds blocked the light of the full moon. He took off his shirt and opened the little jar. He stuck two fingers inside and scooped out the dark axle grease and rubbed it all over his body. He was glad it wasn't chocolate, that would have been disgusting. Then he lifted himself up to the window, tied his shirt around one of the bars, and let it dangle outside. If his measurements and calculations were correct, he would just be able to squeeze his head through.

First, he tried to go feet first. He got his body all the way out, but no matter how he turned or wiggled it, he could not get his head out. He squeezed back into the cell, smeared more grease over his ears, and then tried to go out head first. When he finally managed to get his head out, his body popped out like a bar of soap.

He lowered himself by his shirt to the ledge, then tiptoed around to the back. Enriquito stopped and peeked around the corner. Since the courthouse had been built into the side of the hill, the second-floor ledge was no more than ten feet above the ground. The gap from the building to the hill was too wide to jump, but Ernestina had done her job well. Enriquito scurried across the bouncing branch that bridged the gap, then ran straight up the hill. At the edge of the jungle, he threw himself down on the ground and listened.

The usual night sounds of crickets and the murmur of the sea could barely be heard over the growling and whistling pulsing out of town hall.

Enriquito was scared, his heart was pounding in his chest, but at least he didn't have to sit in jail.

The dark jungle became transparent as his eyes slowly adjusted to the night.

"Boo!"

His heart jumped. Then he saw Ernestina, hanging upside down, right above him, her face glowing like the moon.

She turned off the flashlight. "I hope I didn't scare you." Ernestina jumped down, thumped him on the back, and giggled, "Wow! You're a mess."

Enriquito was covered in a layer of dark grease that had straw, leaves, and dirt stuck in it. He looked like a walking mud man.

He smiled at Ernestina, teeth shining from his dark, greasy face. He was glad to see her, even if she was making too much noise.

"Did you bring the stuff?"

"Yes, but I had a hard time reading your note. It had egg all over it," Ernestina said.

"Sorry, I didn't think Rodolfo would check there, he hates eggs." Enriquito pointed at the moon peeking out from behind the clouds. "We better get going. When those clouds lift, it's going to be bright as day up here."

They climbed up the mountain, silently skirting the ugly brown slashes of cleared land. In the middle of the highest clearing, a bonfire burned, illuminating the surrounding jungle. Ernestina signaled Enriquito to stop. She pointed to the left edge of the clearing; a sleepy worker was leaning on a shovel. The man was staring into the smoldering pile of brush and logs. They skirted the clearing, climbed up the rocky slope, and reached the entrance to the cave. As they slipped into the mouth of the cave, the moon burst out of the clouds and flooded the landscape.

The neon blue moonlight made everything it touched look unreal. They followed the ghostly shadows down to the lake. They cautiously stepped into the moonlight and climbed up on the boulder.

Enriquito searched the shore and found the cayman dozing peacefully. Enriquito pointed him out to Ernestina. "There he is, and he looks bigger than the first time."

"*Que suerte.*" Ernestina shivered. "I was almost his afternoon snack. You can bet that I'll never get in the water with that thing again."

"I have to, for Aurelio—to find out if the treasure is down there." Enriquito was determined.

"Neither of us can go in there," Ernestina said.

Enriquito heard a little tremor of fear in Ernestina's voice. With as much confidence as he could muster, he said, "I think there is a way."

"What do you mean?" Ernestina asked.

"I'll explain later." Enriquito jumped off the rock. Keeping a safe distance from the cayman, he searched the tall grass on the right bank.

"What are we looking for?" Ernestina asked anxiously.

Enriquito didn't answer. He was now on his hands and knees, pushing aside the weeds and looking under bushes.

"Here it is! I think I found it!" Enriquito was squatting in front of a rusty metal stake with a ring on top. The ring had a chain attached to it that disappeared under the grass. Enriquito began to dig like a dog searching for his favorite bone.

"Just as I thought, the box!"

Ernestina jumped in right next to him. They brushed the dirt off the flat wooden surface and then dug around it until they could get their fingers in.

"The treasure, at last!" she whispered.

"No, it's not the treasure," Enriquito said.

"It sure is heavy enough to be a treasure," Ernestina said. She pulled on the thick chain snaking out of the box through a hole on the top.

Enriquito opened the lid. Inside, he found the coiled chain with a very large metal collar attached to the end.

Ernestina held up the collar and looked through it. "It's big enough for a horse," she said. "Look at the workmanship on this. Someone knew what they were doing."

Each of the four curved iron pieces that made up the collar were lovingly crafted and attached by four links of handmade chain. The latch, made of a shinier metal, opened and closed with the precision that only a jeweler's hand could craft. A strong waxy cord attached to a metal loop on the clasp opened the latch when pulled. The cord threaded through the chain, which was thick enough to pull a truck.

"What do you think this was for?" Ernestina asked.

"It was for him." Enriquito nodded at the dozing cayman.

"This is starting to make sense." Ernestina stood up and paced around the box in a circle. "This is where Aurelio went when he snuck out at night! He needed gold for his work, so he made this collar to hold the cayman while he went 'shopping.' The cord opened the latch and the cayman went back to his job, guarding the treasure.

"Aurelio had to be very careful. He knew the Rigols suspected that he had found the treasure and that they were waiting to pounce on him the minute he brought it out."

Ernestina strutted about and asked Enriquito, "What do you think? Am I right?"

"As right as right can be! C'mon. Help me with this." Enriquito coiled the chain and handed it to Ernestina. He held the collar in both hands, testing its weight and balance.

Ernestina saw what he was planning and tried to pull the collar away. "Hold on there, *viejito*, I think I better handle that end of the job."

Enriquito tugged it out of her hands and declared stubbornly, "No! This is my job. You hold the chain."

Ernestina knew there was no arguing, reasoning, or bullying that could move Enriquito when he set his feet in the mud. The best she could do was to make sure no one got hurt.

Enriquito led the way, moving slowly, stepping lightly in the tall grass. The monster lay with his head toward the water, sleepily flicking his tail back and forth as they approached. Ernestina tried to keep the chain from rattling as Enriquito prepared to drop the collar over the reptile's snout. Suddenly, the cayman's eyes snapped open. He hissed like a snake.

Ernestina stepped on the cayman's left paw as hard as she could. She jumped back as the reptile jerked to the left. Enriquito dropped the collar down on the huge head and jumped away. Ernestina pulled on the chain with all her might, until the collar slid back over his mouth and she heard the click of the lock.

To her surprise, the collar did not drop around his neck but cinched tight around his mouth. That cayman would not be dining on anyone until they pulled on the waxy cord that ran alongside the chain and released him.

For an instant, the cayman froze. His tiny reptile brain had no automatic response for this situation. He knew what to do when he saw a fat possum swimming, or how to spin and confuse his victims as he dragged them down to the bottom. This situation required some thinking, and he wasn't wired for that.

Ernestina and Enriquito ran away as fast as they could. They jumped back up on the rock, just in time to watch the cayman's little brain overload.

They looked on in horror as he jumped, rolled, and shook, as if he had bitten down on an electrical cable. His huge tail slapped and splashed a fountain of muddy water. He clawed and dug up great clumps of marsh grass as he strained the chain to its limits. Then, as suddenly as it had started, it stopped. He rolled over on his back and lay on the bank, panting like a large green dog.

"Looks like the chain is holding. Pass me the rope," Enriquito said as he stripped down to his shorts.

Ernestina dug out their twelve-foot diving rope from the burlap bag and handed it to him. They used the rope when they went spearfishing out by the reef. It was their warning system for the sneaky sharks and bold barracudas that would suddenly appear.

Enriquito tied the rope around his waist and calmly nodded toward the cayman. "If he starts acting up again, give it a tug." He winked at Ernestina, who was nervously coiling and uncoiling the rope. Before she could say anything, he dived into the lake.

The cayman heard the splash and rolled back onto his feet. Ernestina watched him straining against the chain, swishing his powerful tail from side to side.

Enriquito surfaced with something in his hands. He wiped off the lake slime and inspected his find. "Look, Ernestina, it's a mask." Enriquito put the golden object up to his face.

"Wow! It looks really old. That's the real thing. I bet it belonged to old Hatuey himself." Ernestina shivered when Enriquito handed her the mask. It was made of the same gold as the locket. Unlike the masks that Ernestina had seen in books and museums, it was not a caricature of a face. It looked as if a soft sheet of gold had been laid down on a real face and then molded onto it.

"Enriquito, it's so real. I feel like he's right here, like he's looking at me."

Enriquito said, "There is more treasure down there," and dived back into the water.

The cayman was now straining every muscle in his body, pulling with all his might against the chain. With this monster pulling on it, the chain looked thinner, almost delicate, to Ernestina. What if this was a bigger and stronger animal than the chain was intended to hold? What if the chain had been weakened by rust?

Suddenly, Ernestina heard a snap! One of the links had broken. The collar was slipping back over the cayman's head!

"Enriquito!" Ernestina yanked on the rope and lunged for the chain, just as the stake came flying out of the ground. She grabbed the stake as it skidded by, then ran, with the chain dragging behind her, toward a small tree growing between two rocks. Her hands were shaking as she wrapped the chain around the tree once and then managed to stab the stake through the loop of chain. Just as the cayman ran out of slack, she let go. The chain snapped tight, sang a high-pitched note, and then pulled the tree down over the lake.

Ernestina ran back to the rope and tugged on it again.

Enriquito looked tiny at the bottom of the lake. The cayman, no more than six feet away, was furiously straining against the chain. It would not be long before the tree snapped or was pulled out by its roots.

Ernestina ran to the boulder and began to haul Enriquito back, tugging on the rope like there was a big fish on the other end. Now he was close enough to shore to stand.

The tree cracked and splintered.

"Up on the rock!" she yelled.

Enriquito's feet hit the rock just as the big reptile propelled himself out of the water. Enriquito was falling backward into the flying jaws when Ernestina clasped his hand and yanked him away. The cayman crashed into the rock just below their feet, then slid back down into the water.

Enriquito collapsed on the rock, trying to catch his breath. Ernestina sat down next to the wheezing Enriquito.

"Enriquito, it doesn't get any closer than that!"

Early the next morning, they awoke to the sound of axes chopping away the jungle. They had spent a sleepless night up in the big tree Ernestina had scouted.

Not more than twenty yards away, a crew of workers was clearing the edge of their grove. Three men cut up the trunks and branches, while four others chopped up the smaller stuff with their machetes. Then they piled everything in the center of the clearing.

One of the men limped back in their direction. Right below them, he took out a large water bottle from a dirty canvas bag, then carried it back to the workers.

Ernestina and Enriquito gathered their belongings and got ready. When the men went back to work, they started to climb down, but the man limped back to return the water bottle. Instead of going back to work, he sat down, pulled out a small guitar, and began to play.

What luck! Of all the trees in the jungle, he had to sit down under *their* tree, the tree Ernestina had chosen to stash their supplies for the escape!

They could hear every word of his song, which he seemed to be making up right on the spot. He sang about a pesky goat that ate everything in its path. When he ate the singer's favorite drum, he got cooked for his crime. The song went on and on, until he ran out of verses. Then, mercifully, he stopped.

The singer looked at his watch and called the workers back for lunch. They sat all around the trunk of the tree, talking and eating. After a short siesta, they went back to work, except for the singer, who picked up the guitar and returned to his song about the many virtues of the goat before and after it was cooked.

"What do we do now, Enriquito?"

"We'll just have to wait. If they catch us, we'll get cooked just like the goat in the song."

They draped themselves over the high branches like lazy lions, and waited for night to fall.

As the sun was setting, the workers gathered their belongings and left. Ernestina and Enriquito groaned when they saw that there was still one bundle left under the tree.

In the clearing, the pile of brush had grown taller than the singer. He was humming and poking at it with a blazing torch, stepping back to watch the flames leap into the twilight sky. Then he picked up a shovel and began walking around the bonfire, shaping it so that he could control it. It was his job to pay attention to the wind and make sure that the hungry flames did not escape and eat up the whole mountain.

"Ay, *Dios*," Ernestina whispered. "He's going to be here all night!"

"We'll wait until the fire gets bigger and he moves to the other side. Then we'll make a run for it."

Unfortunately, it began to drizzle, and the singer returned to the tree. He put on his poncho, pulled his hat low over his head, and settled in for the night. The rain would make the fire sleepy and he knew it could not escape without the wind to carry it away.

The smoke from the smoldering fire drifted all around them and forced them to climb up higher. Below them, the singer snored like a freight train, while they clung to the slippery branches and tried to sleep.

At sunrise, the wet fugitives woke up to the sounds of the workers returning. The singer greeted them sleepily, yawned, and then leaned into the tree trunk and went back to sleep.

"I hope those men finish here and move on soon," Ernestina said. She hung on a branch, stretching and warming her chilled bones in the weak morning sun.

Enriquito was rummaging through the bag Ernestina had packed. He dug out the warm lemonade and a couple of *tamales*. He unwrapped one and felt homesick. "Here, Ernestina, breakfast." He handed her the *tamal*, took a long drink of lemonade, and then passed that to Ernestina.

Enriquito inspected himself for the first time since the escape. His pants and T-shirt were completely coated with a slimy layer of grease, dirt, and itchy leaves.

"What are we going to do, Ernestina?"

"We'll wait. What else can we do?" she replied.

Ernestina found the golden mask in the bag, and then held it up to her face. Looking through Hatuey's eyes, she saw Enriquito looking back with the strangest expression on his face. "Beware, you have defiled our burial ground. If your heart is not true, this worthless metal will bring you nothing but sorrow!"

Enriquito tumbled backward out of sight.

Ernestina took off the mask. "Enriquito, what's the matter with you?"

"Your voice, it scared me," Enriquito answered.

"I didn't say—"

Enriquito put his hand on her mouth to silence her.

The workers had returned to the shade of the tree and were sipping their coffee and passing around a loaf of bread.

The singer took out his guitar. As he tuned up, he asked, "So what's going on in town? Have they found our fugitive yet?"

Enriquito and Ernestina listened closely.

"No, but they know how he got out," a stout *campesino* replied. "The little devil greased himself up and slid out of jail like an eel."

All the men laughed. Then the *campesino* added, "They're saying that the mother sent him to steal the locket. The jar of grease they found is proof that she helped him get away. They arrested her at the bus stop, right when she came back from Havana."

Enriquito almost fell out of the tree when he heard this, but Ernestina grabbed him at the last minute.

The *campesino* continued, "Old Rigol is mad as can be— you know how he is, nobody gets the best of him. He's not wasting any time. The trial is starting today."

Enriquito climbed down lower in the tree, to where their bag was. He swung it over his shoulder and tied the straps tight so that his hands were free. He was ready to climb down.

"Where do you think you are going? You'll get caught!" Ernestina whispered nervously.

"I can't just sit here. I have to go!" He started down the tree.

"Enriquito!" Ernestina hissed. "Alright, you hardheaded little—"

"Ernestina, you don't have to go. She's *my* mother," Enriquito interrupted her.

"How could you say that? I know she's your mother, but she's always been *like* a mother to me." Ernestina put her finger to her mouth. "No more talking."

If they went down the side of the tree away from the group below, they would not be seen, but it would take them longer to get down and there was a chance they would be heard. The quickest way down would be the side that faced the men. Unfortunately, the lowest branch was still a good ten feet off the ground—and right above the group.

Enriquito considered their options, and almost immediately chose the fastest route. Ernestina nodded her approval.

Their escape depended on total surprise. Enriquito studied the spacing of the branches, figured out the fastest path, and then let go. He fell like a pinball, bouncing and swinging downward, almost out of control. Ernestina slid off her branch and hoped for the best.

Enriquito waited for Ernestina on the last branch.

They counted to three, and then jumped, landing right in the middle of the stunned workers.

For an instant, the *campesinos* froze and stared at the strange, dirty little demons that had just appeared in front of their eyes. Enriquito and Ernestina bounced up, a guitar string snapped, and they ran for a gap in the circle of men.

Someone yelled, "Grab them!" But it was too late.

Before they knew what had happened, Enriquito and Ernestina were running down the hill and into the jungle.

"What the devil was that?" said the singer.

Ernestina and Enriquito ran through the rain-soaked jungle until they were back where they had started two days ago, town hall. The branch that Enriquito had used as a bridge to escape was still there.

Ernestina grabbed Enriquito as he started toward the branch. "Where are you going now?"

Enriquito pointed at the building. "In there. My mother's in there."

"What are you going to do when you get in there?" Ernestina asked.

Enriquito threw his hands up and shrugged.

"Don't you think we should have a plan?" Ernestina wasn't used to being the one who insisted on plans.

"Ernestina, my mother is in there. Plan or no plan, I have to go."

Enriquito bolted down the hill and crossed the branch to the ledge. Ernestina took a deep breath and followed him across.

They ran past the window of the cell to the corner of the building. Below them, a group of women was milling about on the steps. If they turned the corner, they would be seen immediately, so they slid back to the cell window.

Ernestina put her hands together to give Enriquito a boost. He shimmied up the bars as close to the overhang as he could, took out their diving rope, wrapped it around his waist, and threw the rest of the coil down to Ernestina.

He counted *uno, dos, tres*; jumped out; and barely caught the edge of the overhang with his fingertips. He hooked his elbows over the edge and heaved himself up onto the roof.

Ernestina was ready when he dropped the rope and braced his feet against the edge. Ernestina swung out, reached for the ledge, and easily pulled herself up onto the roof.

They ran to what looked like a little shed right in the middle of the flat roof and stepped inside. The door had been left open to let the hot air rise out of the building. A tiny circular staircase descended into the dark shaft.

They spiraled downward until they came to an opening in the wall of the shaft.

A steady current of warm air streamed out of the opening, carrying the sound of voices from inside. They ducked into the shaft and followed the voices around a corner. The shaft opened onto a large atticlike space crisscrossed by heavy wooden beams. The voices grew loud and clear as they crawled out of the shaft.

When they looked down, they saw they were no more than fifteen feet above a courtroom. They crawled out and lay down on the wide beam.

They had the best seats in the packed courtroom for the trial of *Señora* Maruri.

Right below them, *Don* Rigol's cousin sat on a black chair in the judge's box, high above the courtroom. The judge was happily reading the comic books strewn about the top of his desk. A gold chain slithered under a pile of comics, a little half moon of gold peeked out from beneath a page. There was no mistaking it. The locket.

Enriquito found his mother sitting to the left of the judge. She looked perfectly calm, with her hands folded in her lap. Enriquito wanted to reach down and pull her up into the rafters and take her away.

At the table to the right of the judge's stand, three men dressed in expensive city suits sat behind three fine leather briefcases.

Don Rigol was strutting around in front of the judge's chair, explaining the nature of *Señora* Maruri's crime.

"As you can see, Your Honor, there is no doubt that this woman conspired to have her son steal the priceless locket that belongs to my daughter, Alysia, and then helped him to escape from our jail."

The judge nodded, giving the impression that he was listening, as he furtively turned the pages of his comic book.

One of the lawyers walked to the table across the aisle and placed a yellow envelope in front of Ignacio. He felt its cover, and then passed it over to *el Viejo*, who opened it and slowly ran his dark, knotted finger over the perfectly white page, mouthing each word silently as he read. When he finished, he whispered to Ignacio.

Apparently, Ignacio had been given the job of defending *Señora* Maruri, and *el Viejo* was helping him. Even though Ignacio was trained as a lawyer, he looked as if he had no idea what was going on.

Along the wall on the left side, there was a raised section with a little rail around it where the jury sat. Enriquito recognized eight of the twelve men. They all worked for the Rigols. It was easy for *Don* Rigol to find men to serve on the juries. Even if they had to listen to *Don* Rigol all day, it was a lot more pleasant to sit inside than to work outside in the hot sun. The best part was that *Don* Rigol would pay them for the day just the same.

The rest of the room was taken up by rows of chairs for spectators.

Alysia and her mother sat in the first row, comparing the nail polish on their perfectly manicured fingernails.

Ernestina noticed that most of the people in the courtroom were related to, or worked for, the Rigols. In fact, the friends of the Rigols had been told to be there at seven thirty, while officially, the time announced for the opening of the doors was eight thirty. But the few in the courtroom who were rooting for *Señora* Maruri were wise to *Don* Rigol's tricks and they had also arrived at seven thirty.

At exactly eight thirty-one, the doors were closed, and even though there were many rows of empty chairs in the room, most of the people who were on *Señora* Maruri's side were left out on the front steps.

Ernestina and Enriquito could hear the group of women chanting outside the courthouse doors, asking to be let in.

They were surprised to see *el Gringo*, the American who bought the sea horses from them. Next to him, a distinguished-looking gentleman in a light suit sat with his Panama hat hooked on his knee. He would occasionally pull a little book out of his pocket and write something down. Ernestina was trying to place the man with the Panama hat. She poked Enriquito and pointed at him. Enriquito knew right away who he was. He whispered to Ernestina, "That's the man from Havana, *el Gringo*'s fishing buddy. We met him at the house."

Ernestina reached into the sack and pulled out a little notebook and a pencil. She opened the notebook and began to write. Enriquito could tell she was trying really hard to make it neat, because her tongue stuck out of the side of her mouth as her pencil scratched across the page. When she finished, she handed it to Enriquito so he could read it.

> DO NOT LOOK UP
>
> LIKE THE NOSE ON YOUR FACE
>
> NEW BOOK—OLD BOOK
>
> THERE FOR ALL TO SEE
>
> HOOK THE BIG ONES
>
> AND THE LITTLE ONE WILL GO FREE

Enriquito read the note, scratched his head, and looked at Ernestina for an explanation. She grabbed the note out of his hand and folded it carefully into the shape of a little fish, and then crawled out on the beam. She stopped above Ignacio and *el Viejo*.

Below her, *Don* Rigol was holding up the little jar of grease that had been found in the jail cell. He was asking *Señora* Maruri if she had ever seen it before.

"Of course, I have seen it before. That's a baby food jar that I saved since my Enriquito was little. I know it's mine, because my little Enriquito was always a picky eater, and that's the only brand of food that he would eat. They don't sell that around here. I have a cousin in Havana who used to bring it to me."

"Tell me, *Señora* Maruri, did you pack your son's dinner the night before he escaped?"

Señora Maruri paused for a second. She had prepared most of Enriquito's meals before she took the bus to Havana. It was Ernestina's job to pack them in the basket and take them to the cell. The chocolate pudding in the little jars had been Ernestina's invention. "Of course, I made all his meals. Who else would do that?"

The women outside managed to open a window. Suddenly, their chanting filled the courtroom. "Let us in . . . Let her go . . . Let us in . . . Let her go!"

"Order in the court! Silence!" *Don* Rigol boomed. He stormed toward the window and slammed it without the slightest concern for the intruding fingers.

This was the moment Ernestina was waiting for.

She took aim and released the note. It twirled and then banked for a landing on *el Viejo's* shiny head. He reached up as if to swat a bug. He trapped the paper fish, and the top of his head wrinkled.

"He's smiling," Ernestina whispered. *El Viejo* had taught her how to fold the little fish to keep her fingers busy when they were sailing home after a day of fishing.

El Viejo opened the fish. He read the note, for Ernestina

to see, then leaned in toward Ignacio and whispered something in his ear.

El Viejo stuffed the note into his pocket. The chanting died down as *Don* Rigol took center stage again.

Don Rigol was having fun acting like a lawyer, hearing himself talk, making believe he was persuading the jury with his logic and wit. It was just a game. *Don* Rigol did not persuade. He *made* people do exactly what he wanted them to do.

The jury seemed restless. *Don* Rigol could see that the chanting had thrown off their concentration. He called for a twenty-minute recess.

Ignacio got up and *el Viejo* led him out of the room by his elbow, whispering in his ear all the way. When they were alone in the hall, Ignacio said loudly, "I cannot believe what you are saying. They have always been very kind to me. They even gave me a job when I lost my sight. If it were not for them, I would be out in the street."

"Ignacio, I understand, but that has nothing to do with what I just told you. Well . . . come to think of it, it has *everything* to do with it," *el Viejo* said.

"What do you mean?" asked Ignacio.

"They gave you the job because you are blind."

"Yes, that is why I am grateful," said Ignacio.

"I mean that they gave you the job because you can't see. You couldn't see that they changed maps and hid things. Ignacio, you did them a favor, not the other way around. You were perfect for the job. I am sorry, my friend, but now we need to help *Señora* Maruri, Enriquito, and Ernestina, because they are in a sea of trouble in a leaky boat."

Ignacio pulled his arm away from *el Viejo's* grasp. He turned to face the wall. For a moment, he did not move. Then he exhaled loudly and followed the wall to the stairs. He walked down one flight to the records office. *El Viejo* followed at arm's length.

In the courtroom, *Don* Rigol was carefully adjusting the handkerchief in his breast pocket. He looked as if he were posing for a portrait.

His relatives and friends were crowded around, complimenting him on his performance. Alysia cut through the group and slid next to her father and said, "Papi, this is sooo boring. How long will it take? I have a birthday party to go to in the afternoon. Can't you just send her to jail and get it over with?"

"Yes, of course, my dear, this won't take much longer." *Don* Rigol stood up and waved his scented handkerchief, and they all rushed back to their seats.

No one had told Enriquito's mother that she could get up. She was still sitting in the uncomfortable wooden chair right below the judge. He was reading his favorite comic book, *Tarzan, King of the Jungle.*

"Your Honor, I am ready to continue," *Don* Rigol proclaimed.

"Yes. By all means, do proceed." The judge waved his hand, barely looking up from his reading. *Don* Rigol paced slowly in front of the judge's throne, making sure everyone's eyes were on him.

"Now to resume. We are well aware that you planned the theft, and convinced your son, an innocent, to carry out the crime. We all know that you employed yet another innocent child, Ernestina, to help carry out your son's escape from jail, and you have defied the request of the court to reveal your son's hiding place."

Enriquito's mother saw that Ignacio and *el Viejo* had not yet returned. She raised her hand and complained, "Your Honor, the twenty minutes are not up. Shouldn't we wait for my lawyer to come back?"

Don Rigol interrupted, "Your Honor, everyone else is here. Let us not waste any more time. *Señora* Maruri, answer the question."

"I am not saying another word until Ignacio returns, and that's final." Enriquito's mother crossed her arms and turned her face away from *Don* Rigol.

Don Rigol's eyes shot out sparks as he watched her settle deeper into her chair. He hammered the railing with his fist. "Who do you think you are to refuse to answer *my* questions!" he yelled. The rafters shook.

Ernestina watched Enriquito carefully. He had crawled out over the courtroom and was crouched like a cat, ears twitching, fingernails digging into the wooden beam. Every muscle in his body was drawn tight, ready to pounce.

Ernestina untied her end of the diving rope and crawled out on the beam behind him. As she stuffed the rope into Enriquito's sack, a pencil rolled out. She reached for the pencil and bumped the sack. The heavy mask slid out and nestled on the back of Enriquito's head. He reached back, but it squirted away. Hatuey's eyes were alive, flashing as the mask teetered on the edge of the beam.

Enriquito made one last stab at it, missed, and slipped off the beam. He was now hanging by the back of his knees, swinging upside down.

The mask clattered into the middle of the courtroom, just missing *Don* Rigol. Screeching in a most unmanly way, he jumped back, landing in the midst of the spectators' section.

Ernestina was barely able to reach the rope, still tied around Enriquito's waist, before he swung off the beam. As he fell, the rope looped itself around the beam and snapped tight when it ran out of slack. Enriquito bounced once and was left dangling, just three feet off the floor, upside down.

The howls and screams of the spectators filled the courtroom. *Don* Rigol tried to stand up and run, but instead, he flew backward into the seated spectators and landed on his wife's lap. The dozing judge fell off his chair, while the lawyers instinctively dived under their table.

El Gringo and the stranger, watching closely from the fringes of the crowd, were the only ones who seemed to be amused.

Señora Maruri was the first to reach Enriquito. She hugged him by the legs and started to cry. She was so happy to see him she even kissed his sneakers.

Alysia ran over to the dangling boy. "Well, well, well, what a wonderful surprise. Our little thief has delivered himself, already gift-wrapped for us."

Ernestina was not about to admit defeat. She wrapped the other end of the rope around her arm and jumped off the beam. Above the crowd, like a crazy circus act, Ernestina was dangling, spinning, while Enriquito swung back and forth like a pendulum.

Enriquito angled his leg to the right and swung left over the judge's stand. He swooped over the pile of comics, hooked the locket with his little finger, and swung off the stand. Climbing, monkeylike, up the rope, he heard Ernestina yell, "Watch out, Enriquito!" They were trying to pry Ernestina off the rope. He knew what was going to happen next. Ernestina put up a good fight. Enriquito had climbed almost within reach of the beam when she let go. The whole courtroom gasped. The rope slithered down with him as he fell, then got caught on a nail. He bounced upward and twirled above the cheering crowd.

El Viejo and Ignacio hurried back upstairs to see what the noise in the courtroom was all about. The women demonstrating on the front steps called out to them as they passed. *El Viejo* opened the doors, and the angry women ran into the courtroom, chanting and carrying signs.

Don Rigol shouted for everyone to leave the room, but no one was listening. He grabbed the foreman's revolver and fired one round into the air.

Boom!

The bullet zipped by Enriquito's leg. The ear-splitting report flattened all the other noise in the room.

"Hey! Are you crazy? You almost hit me!" Enriquito screamed.

"It would serve you right—you little criminal!" The veins on *Don* Rigol's forehead popped out like angry little rivers. "I am going to see to it that you, your mother, and the girl are sent away for good."

The foreman hustled Ernestina and *Señora* Maruri to the front of the courtroom.

Enriquito, still hanging upside down, face getting redder and redder, wanted to speak, but he couldn't get the words out.

Don Rigol glared at Ernestina and *Señora* Maruri. Then he took a deep breath, smoothed his wavy gray hair, and smiled. He looked just like the picture of a smiling devil that Ernestina had seen in a book.

The smiling devil yelled, "We will have order in this court, or I will have it cleared by force!" The foreman and his men stepped menacingly toward the crowd.

"Of course, it would be a pity for you all not to witness the guilty being punished." He pointed to the dangling Enriquito. "After all, isn't that what trials are all about? We punish the guilty to set an example for those who might feel they can break the laws." He looked up at Enriquito. "You'll see, my little friend, no one defies me and gets away with it."

Don Rigol puffed out his chest. "Our greasy little citizen here has stolen my property, escaped from my jail, and disrupted my legal proceedings. We have countless witnesses who will verify that this little urchin trespassed in my daughter's school, ripped a priceless heirloom from her neck, and wreaked havoc in the halls."

Enriquito was dangling over the courtroom like a life-sized marionette, waving his arms and struggling to right himself. Finally, he seesawed his head above the level of his feet, the blood rushed out, and he found his voice. "That's a lie!"

"Silence!" *Don* Rigol yelled.

"That locket was made for my mother by her uncle Aurelio, and then it was stolen out of her house." Enriquito's defiant little voice echoed over the courtroom.

"That is ridiculous," *Don* Rigol laughed. "Your mother's uncle was a crazy man who never left the house. He could not even speak. There is no way he could have made that locket."

Enriquito was kicking his legs and moving his arms

around as if he were swimming in air, trying to stay upright. "You stole that locket, just like you are stealing our mountain—and I can prove it."

Someone in the crowd yelled, "Let him talk!"

Someone else called, "Give him a chance!"

Then Ana, the sculptor, stepped forward and said, "If this is a trial, then he should have a chance to defend himself."

The other women grew bolder and began to chant. "Give him a chance! Give him a chance! Give Enriquito a chance! Give him a chance! Give him a chance! Give Enriquito a chance!"

"Silence!" *Don* Rigol screamed. "I've had enough of this. There is no need to waste any more of my precious time. I have decided, that is, the Court has decided, that he is guilty and he will be punished!" He turned to the judge. "I am sure the judge agrees with me that we should proceed with the sentencing of the accused." *Don* Rigol gave the judge a meaningful look.

"Well . . . I am not so sure. Perhaps he should be given a chance to speak," the judge said meekly.

"Quiet, you fool. I say it's time for judgment to be handed down!" Rigol yelled.

The crowd roared and pushed back at the men who were blocking them. *Don* Rigol raised the pistol and fired into the air. The bullet zipped by dangerously close to Enriquito.

A puff of smoke drifted up from the barrel of the gun, and then billowed around Enriquito's waist.

Enriquito, floating in a blue-white cloud, cried pitifully, "Hey, that was close! I'm just a little kid."

The crowd gazed up in awe at the apparition. Enriquito looked just like one of the painted angels on the ceiling of the town church.

The stranger with the Panama hat, who had been standing off to the side, made his way to the middle of the floor and cleared his throat loudly.

"*Harrumph!* May I have your attention?"

Everyone turned toward the distinguished-looking stranger. Rigol studied him. He decided that he was a respectable man, so he gave him a chance to speak.

The stranger carefully removed his hat and looked around. "I am not from around here," he began, "but from what I have observed here today, I can see that you could use some help."

The stranger nodded at *Don* Rigol. He reached into his coat pocket and pulled out a wallet, opened it, and held it over his head. "I am Chief Magistrate Cardenas. You could say that I am like the umpire at a baseball game. It is my job to make sure everyone plays by the rules. If they don't, I have the authority to step in and set things right.

"It seems to me, if this trial is to be fair, the young man hanging there should be allowed to present his side of the story."

There was a great sigh of relief from the crowd, as everyone exhaled at the same time.

Don Rigol demanded to see his identification.

The stranger handed him a card and his badge. *Don* Rigol glanced at them and said, "It will take some time to properly check your credentials. We shall postpone the trial until I hear from the authorities."

Chief Magistrate Cardenas picked the card and badge from his hand. "That decision, *Señor* Rigol, is not for you to make." Then he handed them to Judge Rigol. The judge knew of Chief Magistrate Cardenas from his student days in Havana, but he studied the badge anyway to buy time. For the first time in his life, he felt like he could make a difference. That thought frightened and excited him at the same time.

When he looked at things simply in terms of right or wrong, like a good judge should, it was amazingly easy to come to a decision. He found his wooden gavel under the comics and slammed it down hard. "I rule that the trial should go on."

The room erupted. The women began to chant. "Free our mountain! Let Enriquito go!"

The judge let the cheering go on for a minute or two, then pounded on his desk. "Silence! Silence! I will not have this disruption in my court!" He liked the sound of that, *my court.* He brought down the gavel again and ordered, "Everyone sit down, be quiet! And for God's sake, get that child down from there!"

Enriquito was lowered, untied, and led to the table where Ignacio and *el Viejo* sat.

The judge asked Ignacio, "Is your client ready to testify?"

Ignacio could see that Enriquito needed time to settle down. He answered the judge, "Your Honor, I have not had a chance to talk to my client. I'll need a few minutes."

"Take your time," the judge said.

Ignacio leaned over to Enriquito and whispered, "You said you have proof that the locket belongs to your family. Can you present it here, now?"

"Yes, I think so," Enriquito answered.

While they whispered back and forth, Ernestina made her way over to *el Viejo* and asked, "Who talked the chief magistrate into coming all the way out here?"

El Viejo looked over at *Señora* Maruri. "When I told her about *el Gringo*'s friend, she took off on the first bus to Havana."

Don Rigol huddled with the lawyers at his table, trying to anticipate the next move. Realizing that Enriquito needed the locket to prove his point, he snaked over to the judge's box.

The judge watched *Don* Rigol's hand shuffling through his comic books. He took aim and banged his gavel down dangerously close to it.

"You are a disgrace to your family name. You will pay for this," *Don* Rigol snarled as he pulled away his hand.

The judge snarled back, "This family has bullied me and everyone else for long enough. We will now see who has disgraced our family name."

Don Rigol changed his tone. In a sickeningly sweet voice, he asked, "Please, my dear *primo*, may I have the locket back? I need it for a moment." There would be plenty of time later to get his revenge.

The judge had no intention of returning the locket, but he searched among the papers and comic books anyway. He could not find it. "It was here, under the—"

"Your Honor, we are ready to begin," Ignacio said as Enriquito led him in front of the judge and then climbed up on the witness chair.

The judge waved *Don* Rigol away from his box and asked Ignacio to begin.

Ignacio's eyes roamed over the ceiling. The whole courtroom looked up to see what he was staring at.

"My client, *Señora* Maruri, is charged with stealing a locket of great value from Alysia Rigol-Betancourt. We will prove that the locket actually belonged to the Maruri family and that it was the *señora*, and not the Rigols, who was robbed."

Rigol stood up and objected, "Your Honor, they will need the locket as evidence, and as we both know, it has unfortunately disappeared."

"Cheaters!" someone called out.

"Quiet!" the judge ordered. "That is true, the locket seems to have disappeared."

Don Rigol bowed triumphantly to the judge's box.

Enriquito watched him strut back to his table, as cocky as the black rooster in the school playground.

Enriquito smiled and stood up. "I have the locket." He pulled it out of his back pocket and waved it around for all to see.

Don Rigol threw his hands up in the air.

Ignacio asked, "What is it about the locket that will prove that it belonged to your family?"

Suddenly Enriquito was aware that everyone's eyes were riveted on him. The confidence he had felt a moment ago began to slip away. All the words and emotions in his head scattered and disappeared. Enriquito looked down at his hands.

Ignacio asked, "Enriquito, why are you so sure the locket belongs to your family?"

Enriquito looked out at the sea of faces. *El Viejo* was squinting at him, like he did when he was looking into deep water. "My mother told me so," he squeaked as he tried to clear his throat.

Don Rigol stood up and protested, "Your Honor, my mother used to tell me that I was the King of Spain, but I am not."

Someone in the audience shouted, "You sure act

like you are!" *Don* Rigol ignored the comment and the laughter. He continued, "If that is what you base your claim on, I'm afraid you do not have much of a case."

Enriquito leaned into the railing. "I dreamed that it opened, there was a note with a red thread—"

"You *dreamed* all this? Please, this is getting ridiculous. Let us stick to the facts. That piece of jewelry has no hinges. It cannot open. Believe me. We have tried," *Don* Rigol blurted out.

"That's because it will open only for the right person," Enriquito said defiantly.

"Well, then, open it!" *Don* Rigol shouted impatiently.

Enriquito looked at the crowd overflowing the courtroom and pouring in through the open courthouse doors. How could he open the locket in front of all these staring faces?

Don Rigol saw the fear in his face. "Maybe this little boy is scared. Maybe he needs his mother to hold his hand. Maybe we are asking too much of him."

Enriquito did not seem to hear him. He was staring over the crowd toward the entrance of the courthouse. The silhouette of a woman standing in the doorway, apart from the crowd, caught his attention. The afternoon light, blazing behind her, prevented Enriquito from seeing her face.

The woman, wearing what looked like a long seashell on top of her head, raised her hand and touched the center of her forehead with her index finger. Suddenly it all came back to him: Aguas Clara on the couch, drawing a shape on his forehead—*If you listen, you will hear me.* Had she already spoken to him?

Enriquito stood up to call out to Clara, but she put her finger to her lips. Then she tapped her forehead twice—*two to remember*—waved good-bye, and stepped out into the blinding light. Enriquito reached out toward the doorway and yelled, "Clara! Come back!"

A hush fell over the room. *Señora* Maruri fainted. Ernestina rushed to help her as everyone turned toward the doorway.

Enriquito looked back at *el Viejo*, his face shining, golden like the mask. Hatuey's eyes flashed, then receded into a black speck flying over *el Viejo*'s head.

Enriquito watched the solitary fly spiral toward the rafters.

All was still inside.

Enriquito traced the spiral, twice, in the middle of his forehead.

Cupping the locket in his hand, he slowly traces the little symbol on the worn face of the locket. Its warmth flows from his arms to his chest and then up to his head.

An image flashes on the back of his eyelids. The cliff is glowing in the afternoon sun. The little blue spiral drifts, pulses, and is gone.

A *click*. The crowd gasps. The locket, opened, nestles

in the palm of his hand. The little roll of paper, with a crimson thread wrapped around it, lies inside.

Enriquito jumped up. "It wasn't a dream!" he yelled. "I did it, I opened the locket!" He held it up for all to see.

Everyone, including *Don* Rigol, had seen the locket magically open by itself.

He strutted nearby, wanting to strike at the curious roll of paper, but he didn't dare get any closer.

Enriquito gently unwound the thread, dropped the paper on the judge's desk, and headed out of the courtroom.

The conga drummer scanned the crowd as he eased into a slow beat. The bass player plucked an occasional note while chatting with the guitar player, who limbered up his fingers by strumming random chords. The piano player practiced scales with his right hand while holding a glass of lemonade in his left. The lanky violinist paced the front of the stage, watching the audience.

Suddenly he turned toward the band, lifted his bow, and counted out, *"Uno . . . dos . . . tres . . . quatro!"*

The conga and the bass laid down a steady rhythm. The guitar and piano jumped in and really made it swing. Floating above it all like a sweet breeze, the violin sang the melody.

Halfway into the tune, the violin player glanced up. The crowd was buzzing, but no one was dancing.

One of the fishermen's wives called out, "This party doesn't start until everybody gets here." Others in the crowd agreed and the music dribbled to a stop.

Then *Señora* Maruri yelled, "Enriquito!" Everyone turned toward the back of the square. The crowd parted and cheered as Enriquito and Ernestina stepped into the gap, followed by the chief magistrate and *el Viejo*. People booed and hissed when *Don* Rigol, looking very miserable and wet, came into view.

Chief Magistrate Cardenas raised his hat, calling for silence, and waited for the crowd to calm down. When he was sure he had everyone's attention, he said, "After studying the original map, I find that the mountain belongs to the people of this town and not to *Señor* Rigol."

First, as the news settled in, there was silence. Then the crowd roared.

The chief magistrate turned and winked at Ernestina and Enriquito.

Ernestina pushed Enriquito forward. He tried to step back, but he froze in the full glare of the crowd's attention.

Someone called out, "Speak Enriquito, say something!"

He saw that it was no use to resist, so he cleared his throat to speak and the crowd quieted down.

"I think the herd of Paso Fino ponies should stay in the hidden valley, where they have lived for hundreds of years."

Enriquito sounded like he was reading a report in class. "Those horses belong to all Cubans. I think we should build a walkway around the top of the cliffs and a trolley to carry tourists to the top. Then we could all look at the ponies anytime we wanted to without bothering them."

Ernestina stepped in front of Enriquito and said, "The second idea we have is to build a museum for Hatuey's treasure. We can display all the beautiful gold objects in cases with little cards that tell their story, just like the ones in the big museums in Havana. Ana, Enriquito, and I could paint murals on the walls that tell the story of the Tainos, Siboneys, and the Arawaks, so people won't forget."

"And we could charge admission," Enriquito added. He looked over at *Don* Rigol and said, "The money we make will go to the town, and we'll decide what it is that *we* need."

The townspeople were bursting at the seams to cut loose and cheer, but Chief Magistrate Cardenas came forward, and instead, they clapped politely.

"All these wonderful ideas are just suggestions. There will be a vote to make sure this is what the town wants. I'll be around to make sure it is done legally." Then without warning, he clapped his hands once and shouted, "This case is closed. Let the fiesta begin!"

The musicians picked up their instruments and began to play.

Ernestina, spinning and waving her arms, danced for the crowd. Then she slid around the conga drums, pulled on Enriquito's elbow as if it were the handle of a suitcase, and swung him to the center of the stage.

As they spun by the piano, she snatched a cup of lemonade and balanced the drink on top of Enriquito's head.

Enriquito watched a glittering smile rising above the crowd.

"Dance!" Hatuey's laughter floated on the melody. "Dance and you will always remember!"

Ernestina danced like she was trying to make it rain, while Enriquito counted beats and did not spill a drop.

About the Author

Enrique Flores-Galbis says, "This book began on a painting trip to Cuba, the place where I was born. While walking in Havana, I heard the ghosts rattling their satchels of memories and bones. They brushed my cheek as they whispered by, breathing color and light back into the crystallized memories of an exile. Now I can return to this magical place any time I want, and be inspired by the sweet perfume of decaying mangoes to write down the stories that the ghosts whispered in my ear."

Enrique Flores-Galbis, at age nine, was one of 14,000 children who left Cuba in 1961, without their parents, in a mass exodus called Operation Pedro Pan. He and his two older brothers spent months in a refugee camp in southern Florida.

He now lives in Forest Hills, New York, with his wife and two daughters. A noted portrait painter and art teacher, this is his first book.